PLEASE

LOVE

ME

KIMBERLY GORDON

Energion Publications
Gonzalez, FL 32560
2013

Cover Design: Henry Neufeld
Cover Art: Josh Green

ISBN10: 1-938434-56-0
ISBN13: 978-1-938434-56-3
Library of Congress Control Number: 2013932754

Energion Publications
P. O. Box 841
Gonzalez, FL 32560

energionpubs.com

Dedication

*To every woman who has ever had her heart broken,
never give up on the love God has planned for you.*

TABLE OF CONTENTS

1

Cincinnati, Ohio

May 1876

"Margaret, are you crying, again?" Paula asked in an exasperated voice. The sour twenty-nine-year-old placed a hand on her hip in a scolding manner. "When are you going to stop dreaming about what could have been? This is reality for you girl, and you had better learn to live with it."

Margaret Roe did not want to hear any more of Paula's preaching. She ignored her roommate and remained still on her little cot.

"You're going to be late," Paula remarked sharply before leaving the room.

Margaret heard the door slam shut. She winced on her pillow, and allowed fresh tears to flow. At last, she was alone. To herself, Margaret admitted that she had been feeling sorry for herself lately. But why not? No one else had sympathy for her. And she was miserable. She had lived and worked in this orphanage now for fifteen years.

Remembering that first day brought back such painful memories. Margaret's father had removed his hat to give her one last embrace before heading off to war. It was the war, between the North and South, the Civil War. Margaret's mother had died shortly after Margaret was born. Gerald had never quite recovered from that loss. So with no other relatives to care for her, Gerald had taken eight-year-old Margaret to the orphanage for their care until he returned. Sadly though, he never returned.

"I'll see you soon, baby. Don't worry about your pa. I'll be thinking of you. I love you," he had said before walking away. Those were the last words she'd heard him say. He was the last person who had ever loved her.

Margaret wiped a few tears away. "I can't stand this place!" she sobbed into her pillow. "I'm sick of it. I want a new life." She buried her face and cried anew.

At twenty-three years of age, Margaret knew her chances for a new life were slim. She had no special skills. She knew how to sew, but not well enough to be a seamstress. She knew how to cook, but only a little. She could be a maid somewhere, but she was already a maid for fifty children. This arrangement was how she kept her room and board in this Cincinnati orphanage. There was a small wage, but what on earth was there to spend it on? Margaret did allow herself the special indulgence of buying sweets at the bakeshop. Eating the confections seemed to be the only happy moments she could make for herself. She knew all too well though that her sweet tooth had led to the thickness in her middle. She still had a womanly figure, but her waist was just not as narrow as other women her age. But her lonely, unhappy life simply kept her returning to the bakery time and time again.

"Maggie, you better get to work!" a voice barked from the other side of the thin door.

"Yes ma'am," she replied, recognizing the voice of the head mistress. Regardless of her dislike for the current situation, she still had to eat and have a roof over her head. Reluctantly, Margaret sat up and wiped her red puffy eyes. "I'll find some way to change things," she promised herself quietly.

Margaret pulled her red wavy hair back into a bun. She fastened it with several hairpins and pulled on one of the two blue uniforms she wore every day. Over this she placed a long white apron. She was ready, by all appearances, but certainly dreaded the day's drudgery. First she would have to help prepare and serve breakfast to the multitude. Then she would have to help wash all those dishes. Secondly, she would tend the children's sleeping quarters, cleaning the privy, straightening the beds, sweeping the floors and changing soiled sheets. Third, it was her job to haul away the dirty laundry to the wash rooms. Her fourth task was to help with the midday meal, but after that, she was entrusted to run errands for the head mistress. This was a tolerable task because it got her outside into fresh air. Upon her return, she helped with supper and then assisted in putting the children down to bed. This final duty was her least dreaded job, because the children, with their innocent smiles and sweet charm, always cheered her. Margaret and the children imagined all sorts of silly stories to fill their minds with something nice to dream about. They enjoyed her stories the best and thanked her with hugs. These small acts of affection helped fill the enormous void in Margaret's heart. But it was still left wanting.

An entire month passed. Nothing had changed. Margaret still cried into her pillow at least twice a week. And at least four times a week, she stopped off at the bakery while running afternoon errands. Usually, she ate one confection right then and there and saved the rest for bedtime snacks. While she was out, Margaret also liked to purchase a newspaper. It was her only connection with the rest of the world, and she had learned to read from her father. She perused the ads for job listings in secret. If word ever got back to Miss Crandle that Margaret was searching for new employment, she would be out on the street for sure. Having to hide her intentions made locating a new job very challenging.

The ninth of June started out like any other day. Margaret completed her morning chores and received the list of errands from Miss Crandle. When she left the orphanage, Margaret made a bee line for the bakery, stopping only once to buy her daily paper. Taking her pastries to a nearby bench beneath a tree, she sat down to review the advertisements. Margaret's mouth stopped mid-chew as her eyes read **Brides Wanted** in bold type. She continued to read: *Mail order agency seeks women of hearty stature to be paired with* *gentlemen on the frontier in holy matrimony. Apply in person or mail inquiry to Simon and Braun Agency, Chicago, Illinois.*

Margaret's mind spun wildly. Did she dare? Could she even consider it? Being a mail order bride would certainly solve two of her problems. She would finally be able to leave the orphanage and possibly, just possibly, she would find love. The thought made her almost giddy. Would she get paired with a man who would love her? Would he fill the aching void inside her heart? But oh, what if he was mean and cruel? She would be giving up one miserable life for another. Margaret stared at the black print. If it were possible, she would have burned a hole through it with her staring. Should she? Shouldn't she? These questions kept repeating themselves in her mind.

Dozens of strangers passed, completely oblivious to Margaret's inner turmoil. The streets were crowded with wagons and carriages, men on horseback, and women running errands with children in tow. The sky overhead was bright with summer's sun, but a soft breeze blew down the street making it a very pleasant day. Within this scene, Margaret's mind finally made a decision. It was worth the risk! Her situation called for drastic action. She was tired of crying into her pillow every night. She was tired of dreading each day. She would do it! She would take her saved money and go to Chicago. Smiling with her whole being, Margaret jumped up from the bench and hurried back to Miss Crandle.

"Have you lost your mind?" the head mistress asked at hearing the news.

"No ma'am. Not at all. I'm quite sane," Margaret answered calmly.

The white-haired spinster tried a new approach. "But Margaret dear, you belong here. There's a roof over your head and plenty to eat, obviously," she spoke with a gesture toward Margaret's waist.

But Margaret stood her ground. She would not yield on this. "Miss Crandle, as you know, I've been here for fifteen years. My friends have come and gone. Most are married now, or working happily somewhere else. I may be twenty-three, but I do not plan to spend the rest of my life as a spinster. This may be my only chance to marry and I am going to take it."

Miss Crandle snorted. She hated to lose such a hard worker. "And just when will you be departing?" she demanded with hands on her hips.

"In three days, on the twelfth."

Miss Crandle's voice was shrill. "That soon? How am I going to train someone to take your place so quickly? You're being quite unfair. I insist you give me at least four weeks. It's the least you can do after all we've done for you."

"Sorry, ma'am. I cannot. I leave on the twelfth. That's the next train for Chicago."

"Mark my words, missy! You'll be back!" Miss Crandle answered angrily. She was completely put out by the girl's determination and confidence. "It must be your red hair. Maybe you just can't help but be bold and unsensible."

On the morning of June 12, 1876, Margaret Roe donned her only non-uniform dress. It was a soft brown cotton, trimmed with a thin strip of crocheted ivory lace. Small buttons enclosed the front up to her neck. It was a simple dress that she usually wore to church. Along with her train ticket, she purchased a new straw hat. Its purpose served more for decoration than shade. A simple brown ribbon adorned the brim.

Margaret patted the bun fastened at the nape of her neck. For the first time in ages, she felt pretty. But maybe it was just her excitement putting all sorts of crazy thoughts into her mind. Her heart was pounding with anticipation of stepping onto the train and beginning a new life. In two short hours, she would be on her way. Margaret grabbed the small carpet bag which held all her worldly belongings.

"Good luck," Paula spoke, poking her head in the door. "I'll probably miss you," she teased, "but not your crying every night."

"Thanks, but I won't be crying anymore," Margaret answered confidently. She gave her roommate a quick hug. "Bye, Paula."

Surveying the small room for the last time, Margaret left the past behind her and walked outside where the children waited to say goodbye. Many wanted a hug. Some just waved. A few had tears in their eyes. It was a touching send off, but Margaret knew she had to go. She bid them all farewell and headed out the gate. As Margaret walked down the street she never looked back, not even once.

Clackety, clackety, clackety… Margaret closed her eyes and listened to the sound of freedom. The train was at full speed, taking all its passengers northwest to Chicago. Only an hour before, they had pulled out of the station at Indianapolis. It was now three-thirty in the afternoon. Margaret couldn't possibly be more excited. She chomped on some bread and cheese she had purchased at the last stop. By ten tonight, she would be in Chicago. Her stomach fluttered with anticipation and the many wonderful possibilities for her future. Her gaze roamed the countryside dreamily as she wondered where the agency would send her. She wondered about her future husband too and hoped that he would be delightfully handsome. For tonight, she would take lodging in an hotel. Tomorrow, first thing, she would find the Simon and Braun Agency. Fleetingly, she wondered how long it would take them to place her out.

After finishing her bread and cheese, Margaret closed her eyes. The gentle rocking of the train car and low hum of voices inside lulled her to sleep. However, by eight o'clock, she was quite hungry and her body was stiff from sitting on the train all day. She looked forward to a good night's sleep in a big warm bed and a delicious meal from any one of Chicago's many restaurants. Margaret had never actually been in an hotel before, but she had heard they were very nice.

Weary travelers peered out the window into the darkness. Finally, lights appeared in the distance. Chicago. When the train pulled into the busy station, Margaret could hardly believe how many people were there, considering the late hour. She grabbed her small drawstring purse and awaited her turn to step off.

At least one hundred people filled her view. Some greeted passengers, others waited for cargo. Some were there to watch, while others in the street were just passing by. Margaret looked at the large train station in awe. Gas lamps flickered light everywhere, like it was almost daytime. But in the distance, she could see many tall buildings.

What an exciting place, she thought. Passengers began to move toward the rear of the train as bags and trunks were unloaded. Margaret found her one small carpet bag and felt a little self-conscious as other women, nicely dressed, claimed much larger luggage. Margaret scanned the crowd for an attendant. Finding one with a trustworthy face near the door to the station, she determined to ask him a question.

"Excuse me, sir," she spoke politely.

"Yes, ma'am. How may I help you?" he asked.

Margaret held back a grin realizing he had mistaken her for a married woman. She was not married, yet ... but soon. "Sir, would you please direct me to a decent hotel?"

The uniformed man quickly surveyed the young woman to determine her social standing. It was apparent by her clothing and sparse luggage that she was working class.

"Try the Brown Hotel or Amberly Inn," he suggested. "Go three blocks down the street, then turn left. They are both on the left side of the street."

Margaret nodded her head in understanding. "Thank you." As she walked away, she repeated, "three blocks down, turn left, on the left." She made her way two blocks down the lighted street when a crowd suddenly began to spill onto the walk. In only a moment it was overwhelmingly crowded.

"What's happening?" she asked out loud to no one in particular. Margaret looked at all the men and women in their fine and fancy attire. The gowns were made of silk with ruffles and pleats and tucks and ribbons and lace. Each dress billowed out in the back over a bustle. As before, Margaret felt a little self-conscious, knowing that her simple brown dress stuck out like a bruised eye among these colorful gowns. Backing up, she stepped partly into the street in order for the mob to pass as they headed to waiting buggies. It was then she noticed the sign for the theater. Apparently, the performance had just finished. Maybe one day she could go to a play. Wouldn't that be fun? Walking on, Margaret found the two hotels.

"May I help you?" a man asked from behind a tall counter at the first establishment.

"Yes. How much are your rooms?" she asked softly.

"Four dollars a night," he answered.

"Does that include a meal?" she inquired innocently.

The man scoffed, looking down his nose. "Certainly not."

Margaret was disappointed, and hungry. "Do you know where I can get a meal?"

"Nowhere close at this late hour," he answered. "Unless you want to go to one of those fancy restaurants up town."

Margaret sighed slowly and considered her options. She was so weary from the long day.

"Do you want the room or not?" the impatient clerk barked.

Margaret nodded. "I'll take it." She opened the string on her purse and pulled out the necessary money. Then she noticed a sign on the wall behind the counter and pulled out another half dollar. "And here's my money for the hot bath," she said, nearly blushing. If she couldn't get a good meal, she could at least get clean. Besides, she wanted to look her best for her interview tomorrow.

The clerk took her money with an exasperated scowl and handed over the key. "Go up to the third floor. Room three-A," he spoke. "I'll be up shortly with your hot water."

Margaret signed her name in the guest register before heading up the stairs. They were covered in a soft red carpet, so her feet made no noise going through the tall corridor. The room was easy enough to find and she entered with relief. The space was at least eighteen feet long; it would be the largest she had ever slept in alone. There were bigger rooms for the children at the orphanage, but she had shared them with twenty other girls.

A large double bed rested near the corner. Next to it stood a small washstand. Beside that was a window, chair and a small desk. A small empty furnace stood in the front corner next to a tall bureau. An old fringed carpet covered the hard wood floor. What luxury this seemed, well worth the four dollars. Margaret placed her bag on the bed and removed her hat. She looked out the window into the semi-darkness before pulling down the shade. As she sat on the bed, fingering the stitches on the quilt, someone tapped on the door. When she opened it, the clerk stood there; his pants were sloshed with water. He did not look happy.

"Your bath is ready across the hall," he spoke and pointed. "When you're done, turn the lever to the left to let out the water." He turned and tromped down the hall to return to his late night post.

Margaret grabbed her key and locked the door to her room. Over in the water closet, a small oil lamped burned on a stool. She shut and locked that door too and leaned over to feel the water. It was wonderfully warm. Not wasting a moment, Margaret undressed and stepped into the tub. The soothing water came halfway up her ribs. Bending her knees upwards, she was able to lower herself all the way to her shoulders. How heavenly this was! After a moment of just being and relaxing with her eyes closed, Margaret searched for the soap. The community bar rested in a porcelain dish on a small shelf on the wall. With it, she vigorously scrubbed, making herself clean and new. Soaking in this quiet moment, Margaret remained in the soothing bath water until her fingers wrinkled like raisins. By then, she was tired enough to fall asleep anywhere.

After drying off with the provided towels, Margaret replaced her clothes. Spotting a basket for used linens, she happily threw in her towel, pleased that this was one basket she would not have to empty.

Margaret returned to her room and changed into her nightgown. After she extinguished the lamp, she cracked her window for fresh air. But before climbing into the bed, she knelt down and folded her hands, offering up a long prayer of thanksgiving. When she was nearly done, she added, "And Lord, please let him love me. Amen." With that, she hopped into bed and fell fast asleep.

When Margaret's eyes opened the next morning, she was wide awake. It was much too thrilling a day to want to lie in bed and snooze, as she had wanted to do so very many times in the past. She leapt up and dressed quickly. After a trip to the water closet, Margaret braided her long red hair and wrapped it in a pretty spiral. After pinning it all to her head, she secured her new straw hat as well. Surely she had to find food next or she would faint away.

Thankfully, there was a restaurant just next door in between the two working class hotels. She ordered eggs, sausage and biscuits. This she washed down with a glass of cold milk, grateful that her stomach was full once again. When she paid for the meal, Margaret asked directions to the Simon and Braun Agency.

"The mail order company?" the manager asked.

Margaret smiled, glad that the man recognized the name. "Yes. The very one."

"It's at the end of Main Street," he answered. "Ask anyone. It's not hard to find."

"Thank you so much!" Margaret smiled in return.

Dropping the handle of her purse around her wrist, Margaret went to find Main Street. It did not take long. She stood outside the doorway to the mail-order company with butterflies in her stomach and a pounding heart. Could she go through with it? Doubt fleeted through her mind, but she pushed it away and stepped inside. It smelled of tobacco.

"Hello ma'am," a gentlemanly voice said.

After Margaret's eyes adjusted to the dimmer interior, she spied a man sitting behind a large desk. He was in his forties with bushy sideburns. Margaret gulped down the nervous knot in her throat. "Hello."

"What can I do for you?" he asked curiously.

With trembling fingers, Margaret opened her purse and pulled out a torn section of newspaper. This she placed on the man's desk.

"I've come because of this advertisement. I wish to be placed on your list of candidates," she blurted quickly.

"I see," he said, looking at her curiously. He then smiled and asked, "Can you read and write?"

Margaret was almost offended. She stood tall with her chin up, answering, "Yes sir. I certainly can." What she really wanted to say was, 'I read your advertisement didn't I?'

"Very well, I'm Jack Simon, glad to be of service," he stated. He reached into a desk drawer and pulled out several pre-printed sheets of paper. "Here are the requirements for our brides and a list of rules. Also listed are criteria for the men involved. Please read them. If you are still interested, sign the first page. Then I need you to fill out the second sheet. We take the answers to your questions and match you with a man desiring your particular attributes and skills."

Margaret winced. "How long does that take?"

Jack Simon shrugged. "We've matched some in just hours, others take weeks."

Weeks? Oh dear. Her money would run out. This was not good news. If it took them more than two weeks, she would be in trouble. She would have to make her seventy-four dollars last as long as possible. Maybe a boarding house would be cheaper than the hotel.

Margaret nodded and took the paperwork to a nearby desk. All the rules and regulations seemed fair. Among other things, the women were required to be faithful to their husbands and the men were required to provide their wife with food and shelter. Margaret signed on the solid line.

The second sheet asked many personal questions. How old are you? Have you ever been married before? Are you a widow or divorcee? Do you have any children? If so, what are their ages? What color is your hair? Eyes? What is your religion? List your skills. Do you have any medical problems? On the very bottom was an open space for additional comments. Margaret answered each question. For the last, she wrote in, 'please place me as soon as possible.'

When Margaret returned the papers to Mister Simon, he asked, "Where are you staying so that we can reach you?"

"The Amberly Inn, right now, but I plan to look elsewhere this afternoon."

The man penned out the name on her paper. "Let me know if you switch," he told her. "So we can find you."

Margaret nodded and waited for more instructions.

Jack smiled at the young woman. "I thank you for coming in, Miss Roe. We will contact you as soon as possible."

Margaret was astonished. "You mean that's it?"

Simon nodded. "Yes. Unless you have any questions."

"I can't think of any right now."

"Then good day to you." He accepted the paper and returned to his work.

Margaret walked out into the blinding sunshine. She could hardly believe it was that simple. All she could do now was wait, cross her fingers, and pray. The town clock struck ten. It was still so early. Maybe she would just wander around town today, taking in all the sights. She would look for a boarding house too.

Margaret strolled aimlessly down one street to another. Occasionally she entered a store to look over the merchandise. There was so much to see. Everywhere she looked, there were people. All the stores were busy. Every street was continuously full of people, horses, wagons and carts going to some destination.

She strolled through the market, surveying the fresh produce and livestock. Margaret had never seen so much food in her life. She kept walking and spied a booth full of tasty sweets. Her favorite! She bought two fruit-filled tarts. Icing swirled in spirals over the top. Remembering the price of breakfast in the restaurant, Margaret retraced her steps through the market, purchasing fresh fruit, bread and cheese along the way. If she bought food here, it would save money.

Margaret decided to return to the hotel with her food. It was too heavy to carry all over town. She ate some bread and cheese at midday before heading out again. Her task now was to find other lodgings. After an hour, she found the right place. *Missus Elsie's Boarding House*, the sign read in big blue letters. Confidently, Margaret walked up the stone pathway and knocked on the door.

"Hello?" a friendly female voice shouted out a downstairs window.

Margaret looked at the woman hanging halfway out. She was in her early fifties and had a very pleasant face. "Hello, ma'am. My name is Margaret Roe. Do you have any rooms?" she asked eagerly.

The woman motioned with her hand for Margaret to come in. She entered the two-story home without delay and glanced around the parlor. It was modestly decorated and seemed a very comfortable place to stay. The lady met Margaret in the front room.

"Hello, dear. I'm Elsie. Sorry about that. I was feeding my cats and just couldn't get out of the room," she giggled.

Once she mentioned it, Margaret noticed the woman's clothing was covered with variously colored cat hairs. "My name is Margaret Roe," she repeated. "I was wondering, hoping, you might have a room available."

The woman frowned. "Not tonight, dear. I'm all full up."

Margaret was genuinely disappointed.

"But I do have one after tonight. Would you like to stay tomorrow?" Missus Elsie asked.

Margaret did not attempt to hide her pleasure. "Oh, I would like that very much," she answered. "How much is your rate?"

"Two dollars a night. Two-fifty if you want breakfast and supper."

"Very good," Margaret stated. "Please put me down for tomorrow."

"How long will you be staying?" Elsie wondered.

"I'm not sure exactly," Margaret replied honestly.

"Can I put you down for one week then? Or two?" Elsie wondered. "Can you guess at all?"

"I guess one week for now, please. It will depend on when they find my husband."

Elsie placed a hand to her breast. "Oh dear! Is he missing?"

Margaret had to laugh. "Oh, no ma'am. It's nothing like that. I'm not married yet." It was easy to see Elsie's confusion. Margaret felt she had to explain. "You see, I have signed up to be a mail order bride. I am waiting for Simon and Braun to match me with someone."

Elsie showed both relief and surprise. "Oh, how brave you are, my dear. Are you nervous at all?"

Margaret answered honestly. "Yes, a little. But I hope and pray for the best. No matter what happens, it will be better than what I had before."

"You poor soul," the woman consoled. After a brief moment, she said, "I will put you down for two weeks. Sometimes these things take a while."

Margaret thanked Elsie for her kindness and left the comfortable home. "Hopefully one day soon, I will have my own comfortable home too," she thought happily. Margaret found her way back to the agency. When she walked in the door, Mister Simon jumped up from his chair.

"I'm so glad you came back. We've found someone for you already," he stated proudly.

Margaret took a step back. "You have?" she gulped. This was it. She could hardly believe it. It had been only five hours since she left.

"Yes. It's almost a perfect match," he boasted. "Please, have a seat."

Wordlessly, Margaret dropped into a chair.

"We just got his application last week. His name is Russell Chadwick. He wants a woman who can read and write. It was also important that his bride know many skills, all of which you listed. He wanted a mature woman with a good head on her shoulders," the man explained.

"Where does he live?" Margaret eked out.

Mister Simon double-checked his paperwork. "Iowa City, Iowa."

Not that far. "How old is he?" He'd better not be over forty, she hoped.

"Twenty-two."

Gracious! Margaret's eyes opened wide. He was younger! She had not considered that. "What does he do?" she questioned.

"A farmer," the agent replied.

Margaret sat still, absorbing all this new information. A farmer, that was a good honest trade. Could she be a farmer's wife? All she knew about farming was growing a vegetable garden.

"Can you be ready to leave tomorrow at eight in the morning?" Mister Simon asked.

Margaret gulped again, but nodded.

"Very good. I will meet you at the train station at eight. The train to Iowa City leaves at eight-twenty," he explained with satisfaction. His commission on this one would be good.

"How much will the ticket cost?" Margaret wondered.

Simon folded his hands neatly before him. "It won't cost you a thing. Mister Chadwick has paid for all your travel expenses and then some," he said. He cleared his throat and handed her a sealed envelope. "This was to be given to the woman we chose to be his bride."

Curiously, Margaret broke the seal. Inside was twenty dollars and a brief note.

Dear woman, this money is for you to spend however you wish. Consider it a wedding gift.

Sincerely, Russell Thomas Chadwick

Margaret beamed with joy. How wonderful he sounded, and how very considerate to send such a thoughtful gift. Her anxiety over this unknown man evaporated. She looked Mister Simon in the eye. "I will see you tomorrow at eight," she assured him. They shook hands on the deal. It was official.

Margaret left in a flutter of happiness. She would meet her future husband tomorrow! Goodness how she wished to impress him. Then she remembered the money. Yes! She would buy a pretty new dress. That would dazzle his eyes and capture his heart. But first, she would have to cancel the reservation with the kind Missus Elsie.

Practically dancing with every step, Margaret entered the ladies' clothing store which Elsie had recommended. They sold pre-sewn clothing in a wide range of styles and prices. She was simply awestruck by the selection. Dresses and gowns in every color imaginable hung on racks. They were arranged according to size, and then by price. She eyed them all wishfully.

"I am Francine. Can I help you?" a dark-skinned woman asked with a strange accent.

Margaret was intimidated. She had never owned a store-bought dress before. "I was looking for a pretty dress," she managed to say shyly.

The woman smiled. "Then you come to the right place. What size you need?"

Margaret shrugged.

"Very well. We find out," the woman said, taking her hand. "Come with me."

The lady led Margaret to a small room. She closed the curtain behind them. "Raise your arms," she ordered.

Margaret obeyed.

The woman took a piece of ribbon, marked off at even intervals and wrapped it around Margaret's waist. As she was adjusting the measurement, she began to poke Margaret's side.

Margaret giggled. "That tickles."

The woman did not look pleased. "You do not wear a corset?" she both stated and asked at the same time.

"No ma'am. I never had to. It interfered with my work," she explained honestly.

The lady looked at her more kindly. "You wear one today? Makes dress fit better. Catch man's eye. Make you look like lady," she added with a wink.

Margaret had to grin. She had never met anyone who talked so strangely. As the woman measured her bust, she asked, "Where are you from, if I may ask?"

The woman never stopped her work, but smiled and answered, "New Orleans. Long time ago I work there in dress shop. Now, I work in mine." Before Margaret could respond, the woman asked, "How much you want to spend?"

"I have only twenty dollars," Margaret replied. It's all she would spend on a dress, anyway. Her own money was for survival.

The lady nodded and left the room. Margaret waited patiently, not knowing what else to do. Finally, after a long three minutes, the woman returned with an armload of dresses and female equipment. "I help you change," the woman offered. "Take off dress, please."

Margaret blushed. She was very uncomfortable changing in front of a stranger, even if it was another woman. Slowly, she reached for her buttons.

"I not see you," the dressmaker spoke kindly. "You have on petticoat? I am Francine, I do this all day."

Margaret removed her brown dress and allowed Francine to fit the corset.

"Tighten your stomach," Francine instructed softly. She pulled the stays tighter. "Too tight? Can you breathe?"

"I can breathe, a little," Margaret replied. Francine adjusted once more. "Better."

"Good. Now which dress you like?" Francine asked.

Placing a finger to her lips, Margaret reviewed her choices. There was a beautiful yellow and white dress, trimmed with ribbons and lace. There were also dresses in peach, baby blue and lilac. Each one was trimmed with varying décor: braid, lace, beads, etc.

"How about the yellow one?" Margaret suggested.

Francine lifted the beautiful dress from the pile. It was a pretty daffodil yellow which fastened down the front with white lace bows. Lace trim outlined the front seams from shoulder to floor. Lace was also sewn along the bottom of the dress, all the way around the billowing train. "Pillow first," Francine then stated. She grabbed what looked like a foot-long pillow and secured it at the small of Margaret's back, just over her rear. "Affordable bustle," she winked. "It makes dress puff out in back. Very pretty. Very stylish."

With Francine's help, Margaret pulled on the dress and fastened the hooks beneath the lace bows. Francine took her to a large mirror. The yellow princess dress fit perfectly. Margaret could hardly believe how shapely she looked or how beautiful.

"You like?" Francine asked with a satisfied smile.

Margaret could do nothing to hide her enormous grin. "It's beautiful!" she complimented. "Wonderful…" Margaret pivoted around on her feet, swishing the skirt and admiring herself for the first time ever. Then and there she made up her mind not to try on any of the other dresses. It would only make her want them too. She could only afford one, so she turned to Francine. "I'll take it!"

"Want to wear now?" the woman asked.

Margaret shook her head. "Oh, no. It would get dirty."

"I box it for you."

"How much will it be?" Margaret worried.

Francine calculated the figure in her head. "Dress and corset, and bustle, is twenty-two dollars."

Margaret nodded. It put her two dollars over-budget, but what was two dollars when this was the outcome? It was well worth it. She could certainly throw in some of her own money to make a good first impression on Mister Chadwick. Margaret left the store ten minutes later feeling like a brand new woman.

It was late in the day now. Margaret returned to her room very weary from all the walking she had done. She sat comfortably in a big chair, eating some of the food she had purchased in the market. Quickly, she grew tired and decided to go to bed early. She wanted a good night's sleep before the big day. She changed into her comfortable nightgown, and after praying, climbed into the soft bed eager to dream about her future.

It was a restless night. Margaret tossed and turned, unable to stop thinking about Russell Chadwick. Her mind spun with questions. What would he look like? What would he be like? What would his home look like? What would the land be like? What kind of animals did he have? How would he treat her? Would he love her? That last one concerned her the most. It was her greatest need.

When morning finally arrived, Margaret was both upset and grateful. She was upset with herself for getting so little sleep, but glad the day was here so she could get up and stop fretting about the unknown. With tired body and sleepy eyes, she dressed in the lovely yellow gown. It took several tries to lace up the corset correctly, but she managed. She brushed out her long tresses and wound them into a large bun at the back of her head. After splashing a little water on her face, she ate some fruit. It was all her stomach could handle this morning. Margaret packed her bag quickly and left for the station with nervous energy.

Mister Simon was waiting for her as arranged. She walked up to him and waited. He looked at her, tipped his hat, then looked past her down the street.

"Mister Simon, it's me, Miss Roe," she spoke gently.

Simon's eyes nearly popped out. He took a step back and gave her the once over. "I say, Miss Roe, you look lovely. I didn't recognize you in that pretty yellow dress."

Margaret smiled. It was the first compliment she had ever received from a man. "Thank you, sir."

"Mister Chadwick is a lucky man," he said under his breath. He regained his composure and reached for something in his pocket. "I have your ticket here. The train will take you to Davenport, then on to Iowa City. Mister Braun wired ahead yesterday. Russell Chadwick is expecting you," he explained.

Margaret took the ticket, feeling very good about herself. Yes, this had been the right thing to do. She had no regrets.

Mister Simon continued. "The trip should take most of the day. Seven hours travel time, plus stops. That will put you in to Iowa City about five o'clock in the evening." He paused briefly. "Can I take your bag?"

"Oh, yes, please," she stated. Margaret stood on the wooden platform and watched as he handed her bag to a crewman. It was placed inside one of the cars. Mister Simon then returned.

"You have fifteen minutes before the train pulls out. Would you like to board now, or stay and chat?" he asked. He hoped she would stay and chat. He was not the only man who had noticed the healthy red-haired beauty. Yesterday, she had been plain, but today, not at all.

"I think I will board," Margaret replied. She was excited about the whole idea and ready to get on the train. "Thank you for everything sir," she spoke, offering Mister Simon a handshake.

He eagerly took it, but instead of shaking it, bent forward and placed a gentle kiss on the warm skin.

Margaret felt a warm blush fill her cheeks.

"Thank you, Miss Roe and good luck," he spoke sincerely. "And if you ever need anything, please feel free to contact me. I am at your service."

Margaret didn't quite know how to take his attentions. "I will remember," she promised. "Thank you for the offer." She pulled her hand away before anyone else turned to watch them. As her foot took the first step onto the train, she hesitated. There was no going back now. This journey would seal her future. Bravely, she went inside. After that first step, the rest were easy. Margaret found a good seat near the window. Today's trip would be a journey full of daydreams.

As the train pulled into the station at Iowa City, Margaret strained to see the people waiting at the depot. Would she see him first and figure out who he was? There were quite a few men standing around. Some were too old, others too young. Only a handful were possibly twenty-two. Margaret jumped in fright as the train whistle blew overhead. The iron horse slowed to stop. Margaret's heart beat wildly. Her throat was dry...

The passengers began to exit the train. Margaret walked slowly toward the steps. Standing in the doorway, she took a deep breath and closed her eyes.

"Please, love me," she whispered, then stepped off the train.

Margaret waited as other passengers went about their way. At last, she was the only woman left standing on the platform. Where was Russell Chadwick? Had he changed his mind? A bead of sweat slid down her back. Margaret was not only nervous, but also very hot.

"Are you Miss Roe?" a male voice asked from behind.

Margaret spun around. A young man in his early twenties stood before her, hat in hand. He was tall and thin with blond hair and tan skin from working hours in the sun. A light brown mustache topped his upper lip.

Margaret nodded nervously. "Yes. Are you Mister Chadwick?" she replied.

He extended his hand in greeting. "Yes. How do you do?"

Margaret smiled, noticing his green eyes and attractive build. He was more handsome than all her daydreams had envisioned. "I am well, thank you."

He looked a little nervous and shifted from foot to foot. Russell searched his mind for something to say. He had rehearsed the entire morning. How surprised he was to see such a healthy young beauty waiting to be his wife. He had expected her to be grossly unattractive. Why else would she be willing to become a mail order bride? It would have to mean that her prospects at home were either slim or non-existent.

"Uh, did you have a nice trip?" he managed to say.

"It was pleasant. Thank you." Margaret wondered why such a good looking man would send for a mail order bride. Surely he could find a nice young lady in town. He was so young too. Most men didn't want to be married at twenty-two. And it was so much more socially acceptable for a man to be single at that age than it was for a woman.

After an awkward moment of silence, Russell asked, "Is that your bag?"

Margaret nodded. "It is."

"How many trunks do you have?"

"None."

The man seemed genuinely surprised. This woman, covered with volumes of yellow material and lace, appeared as though she would come complete with trunks full of fancy dresses. He was a bit thankful at the news though, for there was little need for pretty clothes on a farm. It required hard work from sun up to sun down.

"Are you ready to go?" he asked, grabbing her single baggage.

"Ready as ever," she tried to answer lightly.

Margaret followed as Russell led the way to his wagon. After placing her bag inside, he assisted her onto the seat. Climbing up, he said, "We'll go straight to the Reverend first."

She was surprised and said so. "So quickly?"

He looked at her frankly. Margaret was slightly uncomfortable staring into the depths of his green eyes. "If we're sleeping under the same roof tonight, we'll do it right. I'll have no one snickering behind our backs," he explained, flicking the reins.

Margaret blushed to the tops of her ears. Of course they would have to get married right away. She had heard about what happened on the wedding night, but honestly, he didn't have to put it so bluntly. They had only just met. At least he was a moral man...

As they rode through town, Russell tipped his hat to everyone they passed. Each person stared in wonder. Margaret surveyed the community; it was larger than she had expected. There were dozens of official business looking buildings, and dozens of homes. She could smell suppers cooking from kitchens. It made her hungry. Past the town, Margaret could see fields of grasses and oak trees that dotted the landscape.

"How far is it to your home?" she asked, making small talk.

He pointed south. "About five miles that way, along the Iowa River."

"What's your place like?"

"Run down right now," he confessed with a sigh. "I just bought it back in April. All I've had time to do is work in the field."

Margaret said nothing, waiting for more information.

"There's about twenty-five square miles in all. The house overlooks the river."

"It sounds lovely," Margaret answered with a smile. After this information, she grew more excited about her new home.

Russell brought the buggy to a stop in front of a small pretty cottage. Flowers reached for the sun beside a short picket fence. "This is Reverend Grady's place. You'll like his wife," he assumed with confidence.

Russell reached for Margaret's waist, assisting her from the wagon. They walked up to the door and knocked. Margaret's knees were practically knocking too. She was so nervous, not only about the marriage, but also about tonight.

"You're here!" a pretty woman exclaimed as she opened the door. "Jack, Mister Chadwick is here with his bride," she hollered back into the house. "Come in, come in. Welcome!" she greeted them. "How do you do?" she asked and extended her hand to Margaret. "I'm Susan Grady."

Margaret extended her hand. Susan Grady seemed very kind. Her abdomen stuck out heavy with child. "I'm Margaret Roe," she returned. "It's very nice to meet you."

Susan returned her smile and looked at Russell. "Mister Chadwick, what a beauty you've captured."

Margaret was very embarrassed by having this said in front of Russell. She was not at all used to kind words or compliments. She looked toward the floor quickly and noticed Susan's bare toes sticking out from beneath her skirt. She soon forgot her embarrassment at the amusement.

Another man entered the room. "Good to see you, Russell. Right on time too," he said looking at the clock on the wall.

"Hello Jack," Russell greeted, obviously friends with this man. They shook hands. "Jack, I'd like to introduce you to Miss Margaret Roe, my intended."

"How do you do, miss?" the Reverend asked in a friendly tone.

With a shaky voice, Margaret answered, "Very well, thank you."

Reverend Grady cleared his throat. "Are you ready?" he asked the couple. He then grabbed a Bible resting on a nearby table. He opened the well-worn pages and began reading from Ephesians, chapter five. When the verses were complete, he began the wedding vows.

Margaret felt like she was in a dream. She spoke her vows when instructed. Russell spoke his in return. It was over quickly and efficiently. There were no rings involved.

"I now pronounce you man and wife," the Reverend announced. He gave Russell a wide grin. "You may kiss your bride now."

Margaret gulped. She looked at Russell. He gently placed a hand on her shoulder. His touch was very light. Margaret closed her eyes as his face came near. This was the moment she had thought of a thousand times. Her first real kiss.

Russell leaned forward and placed a respectable kiss on Margaret's cheek. After the brief touch, Margaret opened her eyes. Was that it? She was greatly disappointed that he had not given her a real bridal kiss. Maybe he was just too shy to kiss her in front of the Revered and his wife. That had to be it.

Susan Grady giggled with delight. As best as she was able with her large stomach, she gave Margaret a warm hug. "Congratulations!" she spoke lively. "You've got the best bachelor in the county."

Forgetting her disappointment, Margaret smiled. "Thank you, Missus Grady."

"Oh, call me Susan. I hope we will be good friends," the kind wife said happily. Susan brought her hands up to her mouth. "I almost forgot. Wait here."

Russell and Jack chatted freely while Margaret waited for Susan to return. The wait was brief. Susan emerged from the adjacent kitchen carrying a large basket. "I have supper all ready for you. I knew you wouldn't have time to fix anything," she explained.

Margaret took the basket. "Oh, Susan, thank you so much. How thoughtful you are." Margaret was glad that she had a friend already. It eased her anxiety about the decision to leave Cincinnati.

"We better be going," Russell said to his friend.

"Missus Chadwick, are you ready?" he then asked politely.

Margaret looked to Susan, then to her new husband. "Yes, Mister Chadwick, I am."

Russell took the heavy basket from her arms and led the way back to their wagon. Again, he helped her onto the bench. "See you Sunday," he called out to the Gradys. "Thanks for the meal, Susan." With that, he slapped the reins, made a noise in his mouth, and the horses were off.

The sun was still well above the horizon, but the air was not as warm as it had been on the train. Margaret took a deep breath. "The air smells so good and fresh out here, not like in the city."

Russell smiled. "Wait 'till it rains. That's when it smells the best."

Margaret returned her gaze to the countryside. She saw several houses, some planted fields and open grasslands. The land was very beautiful with gentle rolling hills and large shady oak trees. The river flowed by quietly, glimmering in the sun.

"Missus Chadwick, I'm wondering, are all your dresses that, uh…frilly?" he asked.

Margaret looked down to the floorboards. If only he knew she was still wearing her work boots beneath this dress. He would not have asked that question. "You can call me Margaret, or Maggie, if you like," she suggested.

"Alright Margaret, do you have any practical clothing?" he rephrased his question.

"Yes. This is my only pretty dress."

Russell's sigh was a little too obvious. "That's good," he answered. "You wouldn't want to ruin all your clothes on a muddy farm."

Margaret wasn't sure how to take his comment. He had not exactly complimented her at all about the dress, or her appearance. His question hurt her feelings. They continued on in silence for quite some time. Maybe it's just nerves, Margaret thought. He probably didn't mean anything by it.

Russell sat brooding as his wagon rolled on. He could kick that man at the agency in Chicago for sending such a pretty girl. It was not at all what he had wanted. He'd needed a sturdy, hard-working, ugly woman to help him on the farm. It would have made his plan so much easier. Regardless, she was here, so he was determined to make the best of it.

Margaret decided to try conversation again. "What should I call you?"

He shrugged. "Whatever."

"Do you prefer Russell, or Mister Chadwick?"

Unemotionally, he responded, "Russell is fine."

"Very well, Russell. I just want to thank you," she spoke boldly.

He looked at her oddly. "For what?"

Margaret gave him a small smile. "For giving me a chance at a new life."

Russell nodded. "Think nothing of it. Say, did you get the envelope of money?"

Margaret debated telling him how she had spent it. He made such a stink over her beautiful dress only moments ago. "Yes, I did. Thank you," was all she said.

Again, silence as they rode the last mile home. Finally, Margaret saw a small two story house in the distance. The wooden structure seemed to lack care. A barn nearby seemed as large, or larger than the house. Corn fields stood in neat rows behind the structures. The river bordered the property on the east side about two hundred feet from the house. Margaret bit her bottom lip with worry.

Russell noticed her troubled face. "I told you it was run down. The previous owner was very old and couldn't take care of it. When I moved in, planting was my first priority," he explained. "Right now, I'm working on the barn. It still needs a new roof. See the holes?" he asked while pointing.

He pulled into the yard, set the brake, and jumped to the ground. He walked around the wagon to help Margaret. She was staring at the house. "Welcome home, Missus Chadwick," he said, trying to sound cheerful. After grabbing her bag, he waved one arm toward the house. "Shall I show you around?"

Margaret looked at the broken step leading to the front porch. The structure certainly needed work. They entered the door. The bottom floor was divided into two long rooms. The stairway ran up the middle. To the left was the combined dining area and kitchen. To the right was what might be considered a parlor.

"I'll show you your room," he spoke gently.

Margaret furrowed her brows. "My room?" she repeated.

He led the way upstairs. The landing at the top was very small. There was a door to each side. He opened the one on the left. "This is yours," he explained. He entered and placed her bag on the bed.

Margaret entered and looked around. There was one large window on the opposite wall. The room contained a bed, dresser and washstand. The ends of the ceiling slanted toward the front and back of the house. Margaret was a bit bewildered by the arrangement.

"I know you have questions, but let's eat first," Russell stated. He left the room and descended the stairs.

Margaret lingered within the very plain room. It almost reminded her of the shared room in Cincinnati. At least this one was all her own, and with a little effort, she could make it nice and pretty. She walked across the bare wood floor to the window. Several oak trees protected the house and in a side yard, she saw the remnants of an old clothes line. Past that, a small graveyard sat quietly. It contained only three headstones.

"Are you coming, Margaret?" Russell called from below.

She found him waiting at the table. He had already unpacked the basket from Susan, eager to be fed. Russell offered a pleasant smile. "Susan sent a good meal. Are you hungry?"

Margaret nodded. "Actually, yes." She took a seat at the square table.

Russell gave a brief prayer of thanks before the meal. Only half listening, Margaret said a silent prayer of her own. She prayed for courage and guidance.

"This ham looks great," Russell spoke excitedly. He offered her a thick slice. "How many biscuits do you want?"

She looked at the big flaky rounds. "Two please."

Russell placed two on her plate, then spooned out peas and baked apples.

"This does look wonderful. I only ate some cheese and bread on the trip today," the new wife confessed.

Both adults dug in and ate heartily. Margaret however was unable to eat all on her plate for her corset was laced too tightly for a big meal. Russell polished off his food, then pushed the plate away.

"I guess you're wondering about the separate rooms," he said.

Margaret smiled timidly. "It did cross my mind."

Russell scratched his mustache. "I just figured you would like some privacy. Since we are strangers, I don't expect anything...like sharin' a room. You understand?"

Margaret was floored. He was talking about... oh, she was so embarrassed. Her initial hurt about being put in a separate room was alleviated by the fact that he was giving them time to get to know one another. How very gentlemanly of him. "That's kind of you," she commented shyly.

"You can do what you want to your room. The whole house for that matter," he explained. "If you want, make a list of things you need and we'll go into town together in a few days. I'll be out working in the field or in the barn most days until harvest," he continued.

"When is that?" she asked.

"In about three months," he answered. "My brother Henry will come and help with the harvest."

Margaret's interest was piqued. "Oh? Does he live here too?"

Russell shook his head. "No. He lives back at home."

"Where's that?"

Russell made a strange face. "In Wheaton, just outside Chicago."

Margaret noticed that Russell was looking out the window wistfully. Maybe he was homesick. "Is that where your folks are?"

He continued to gaze outside. "That's where everyone is." He stood up quickly. "I've got work to do before dark."

Margaret watched as he left without another word. She wasn't quite sure what to think of him yet. He seemed kind enough, but there was something strange about him. He was guarded, a little distant. He had not asked her any personal questions at all and he barely looked her in the eye. Maybe he was just a little timid too. Margaret dismissed these thoughts and busied herself with cleaning the kitchen. She decided this was a big adjustment for the both of them. It would just take time.

Russell did not return until dark. By then, Margaret was exhausted from the long day. While he was away, she had taken inventory in the house. The parlor was nearly bare. None of the windows had curtains and there were no rugs on the unswept floor. Tomorrow, she would tidy up. Weary, Margaret was waiting for him in the only parlor chair.

"Are you asleep?" he spoke softly.

Margaret opened her eyes and looked at him. It was apparent he had been pitching hay. Small pieces were stuck to the sweat on his neck. His shirt was open partly, exposing soft brown curls of hair on his chest. Margaret gulped at the sight. Maybe, in a small way, she really had wanted a real wedding night. "I'm awake," she whispered.

"This is your home now, Margaret. You can go to bed any time you want," he explained.

"I was waiting up for you."

He gave her a half-smile. "That's sweet. I will probably go to bed soon myself."

Margaret wanted to talk to him, or just be near him. She waited as he did something in the kitchen.

Russell reappeared and went to the stairwell. "Ready?" he asked.

Nodding, Margaret stood and walked to him. He allowed her to lead the way. She stopped at the small landing and turned to him. Margaret searched her mind for something to say. Maybe he would kiss her good night, on the lips.

Russell watched her shapely figure from behind. The yellow gown fit well, she was plump, but nicely so. He thought her red hair was pretty too. Under his breath, he cursed that Chicago company again. This woman was going to make it more challenging to stick to his plan. He could do it though. He could.

"Good night, Margaret. Sleep well." Russell reached for his door.

Margaret was disappointed, but resolved her heart to be patient a little while longer. "Good night, Russell. See you in the morning."

Crickets chirped noisily in the grasses. Margaret lay in bed trying to sleep. She took deep breaths of fresh country air coming in through the window. After a time, her troubled emotions settled and she fell into a deep sleep.

Margaret arose early. The roosters had yet to crow even and it was still dark out. But she was used to getting up early and wanted to make a good impression today. She stretched and yawned in bed as her gaze wandered around the dark room. It had potential, and thankfully, the bed was comfortable.

After splashing cool water on her face, Margaret dressed. Today there was much to be done, so she decided to wear one of the blue work dresses. Margaret spied the corset resting on the dresser.

Should she wear it today? It would make it difficult to breathe and move about, but still, she wanted to look attractive for her husband. After much debate, Margaret decided to wear the devise, but not to lace it tightly. She braided her hair quickly, letting it hang down her back. That would at least keep it out of her way.

Happy to make the most of her new home, she headed downstairs. Margaret walked softly on the stairs so she wouldn't wake her sleeping husband. She hoped to surprise him with a good breakfast. She lit a lamp and quietly snooped around. There were four biscuits left over from the night before. Spotting a small container of honey in the cupboard, she set it on the table. A tin-full of ground coffee sat on a side table. Taking a pot, she set water to boil on the stove. "Now, what else can I make," she asked out loud. There was only so much she knew how to make. Eggs! That would be easy. Margaret grabbed a linen towel and headed out the door to the hen house.

The pink and blue sky of morning was just moving in from the east and birds sang sweet songs from their perches. An old rooster watched her from the top of the hen house, too lazy to crow. In a pen full of black mud, there were several slumbering pigs. A small breeze blew in air from the horse stalls. It was considerably strong. Margaret managed to gather four eggs, which was certainly enough for two people. She was halfway through with breakfast preparations when Russell came downstairs. He inhaled the smells of morning and smiled.

It was certainly a pleasant surprise to find Margaret hard at work. That red-haired dressed up woman of yesterday hardly seemed the type to be up and going before daybreak. He watched her as she leaned over the stove to make coffee. At least today she was wearing a sensible dress that was anything but flattering. "Good morning," he spoke sincerely.

Startled by his voice, Margaret nearly dropped the pot of coffee. After regaining her composure, she greeted him. "Good morning, Russell."

He tried to see past her to the stove. "What's cooking?"

She spun around quickly to flip the food before it burned. "Eggs," she replied. "And biscuits with honey and coffee."

He raised an eyebrow at the sound of such a heavenly breakfast.

Margaret misinterpreted his expression. "I hope you aren't angry that I fixed this without asking first."

Russell attempted to calm her shaky nerves. "It's quite all right. I want you to feel at home here. In fact, I am quite pleased that breakfast is waiting for me. I'm not used to good meals," he admitted with a straight face.

Margaret exhaled and smiled. It was the first real compliment he had given her. She was encouraged. As they sat down to eat, she stated, "I don't know what you've been eating. There's hardly anything here."

He shrugged. "I catch food here and there. You can see why I'm so thin," he joked.

Margaret laughed a little. He certainly did need filling out. She began timidly, "Would it be too much to ask if I wanted to go back into town today? I would like to buy some food and staples at the store. Plus some fabric for curtains."

Russell thought for a moment. "I have work to do this morning, but I guess I could spare the time in the afternoon. Or, if you'd rather, you could go yourself."

She considered it. If she went by herself, she could return the basket to Susan and take her time shopping. It was a good idea. "I'll go myself. Are you sure you don't mind?"

"That's fine. Just gives me more time to work on that barn roof," he answered. "I'll leave some money for you on the table after breakfast."

Margaret smiled her appreciation. "One more thing...where's your broom?"

Russell swallowed the food in his mouth before answering. "Don't have one."

Margaret raised her eyebrows. "You mean this place hasn't been swept in three months?" she asked incredulously.

"Longer than that actually," he answered with a crooked grin. "It sat vacant all last winter."

Margaret just could not believe it. No wonder. "In that case, can you spare some hay? I'd like to make a broom."

Russell waved his hand toward the barn. "Help yourself."

In her head, Margaret silently reviewed all the things that they needed. "Do you have pen and paper I can use?" she questioned.

"Sure. It's in my room. I'll get it for you," he offered.

When Russell returned, he brought not only the pen and paper, but also twenty dollars. "Do you think this will be enough to cover expenses today?"

It was much more than she had expected. "Yes, plenty. Thank you."

Russell sat down and resumed eating. Margaret ate and wrote out her list. She paused to ask a question. "Do you have any meat in a smokehouse?"

He shook his head. "I can butcher a hog for you, but I can't get to it until tomorrow."

Margaret added beef to the list. After completing her task, she began noting a list of chores that needed to be done. It dawned on her to ask Russell his expectations. "Russell, I need to know what you expect of me. Are there any specific tasks you need me to do?"

The younger man leaned back in his chair. "Take care of me and the house, Margaret. That's all I ask really. If you like animals, you can help me every now and then. They need food, water..."

His expectations were very reasonable, although it sounded like she was just going to be a maid again. Regardless, taking care of one person was mountains easier than taking care of fifty children. She had only one more question. "Russell? Do you want me to clean your room when I clean the house?"

"Might as well. It needs it. Just don't go through my desk, please. I've many personal papers in there."

She nodded. "Certainly. I would never go through anything without your consent."

Russell stood and stretched. "Then we're gonna get along just fine. Breakfast was good. I've work to do now. Let me know when you need the wagon." He grabbed his hat from a peg near the front door and walked out.

Margaret watched as he left without so much as a goodbye or have a nice day. He was kind enough, not cruel at least, but not too affectionate. She sighed and resolved herself to stay busy with work. There was so much that needed to be done.

3

August 1876

Two months went by. Margaret and Russell went through their daily routines without falter. As promised, he worked outdoors most of the day. Meanwhile, Margaret had performed miracles with the house. It was now white-washed with pretty blue calico curtains in each window. The pantry was stocked full, as was the smokehouse. A new clothes line was strung through the side yard and new boards were nailed securely to the front steps. Two rugs partially covered the parlor floor, which now held several new items of furniture. Her room too, now held a chair and new bedside table. Slowly but surely, the house was coming along. And every night it was the same thing: a "Good Night" at the top of the stairs before entering separate bedrooms. Russell had not even tried to kiss her again, much less offer a hug or hold her hand. She was beginning to feel very self-conscious. The thought even crossed her mind that Russell found her undesirable. Day by day, her resolve to be patient grew weaker. Margaret's heart and soul needed love and attention. She was starved for human compassion. What little she did receive came from the minister's wife, Susan. They met once a week as Susan taught Margaret much needed skills. Margaret learned how to cook, make butter, make soap, de-feather fowl, knit, embroider and weave baskets from prairie grass. After having been burned, she even learned how to make a sun bonnet. Susan made a point to tutor Margaret from Proverbs thirty-one, teaching her the qualities of a good wife.

The thing that bothered her most though was the fact that she and Russell went to church every Sunday. He acted like a happy newlywed in front of everyone, when in truth, he practically ignored her. He never asked questions about her former life, her origins, her parents, or anything. He was never cruel to her, just indifferent. Margaret prayed for guidance and understanding every night.

One morning in mid-August, Margaret sat at the kitchen table, crying into her cup of fresh milk. Russell had already gone out into the fields, checking the corn which now grew as tall as a man. Harvest would come soon. Over her sobs, Margaret heard a strange humming noise. She stopped crying and concentrated on the noise. That's when she heard Russell's shouts. "Locusts! Margaret, shut the windows, shut the windows," he repeated.

Margaret stood and ran to the side window. Russell was practically pushing animals into the barn. Margaret saw what appeared to be a dark cloud moving through the blue morning sky. It was an enormous moving mass of flying creatures. Locusts!

Immediately she ran from window to window, closing them tightly. She took the stairs two at a time to get to the upper floor. After she closed the last one, she heard the front door slam shut. A long string of expletives spewed from Russell's mouth. She waited on the upper landing until he had finished. When Margaret descended the stairs, she found her husband propped against a window frame staring into the fields. Tens of thousands of the small flying creatures descended upon the crops. Some even landed in the yard. The chickens seemed quite excited. They fluttered around wildly pecking at the free meal.

Margaret tentatively placed a consoling hand on Russell's shoulder. It was the first time she had ever reached out to touch him. "I'm so sorry," she spoke softly. "You've worked so hard. Will they eat everything?"

Russell took a deep breath before answering, "Probably."

Margaret was thankful that he had not pulled away from her touch. "How long will they stay?" Her thoughts had come too soon.

Russell pulled away and removed his hat. He smacked it against his open palm. "Maybe just one day, maybe a week. There's no way to tell," he answered angrily.

Margaret peered out the window again. She thought of their cow, their two horses, and the pigs. "Will they hurt the animals?"

"No." His voice sounded dejected.

Margaret tried to think of a way to help him. Of course, there was nothing she could do. "Do you want some coffee?" she offered weakly. "I had planned to make a blackberry pie later this morning. We can have that with dinner." She hoped this would give him a little something to look forward to.

He only grunted and nodded. Margaret took this for the affirmative. She set out to find the coffee pot. Little did she know that this was the start of a very long, hot, miserable week. The locust plague lasted five entire days. Russell and Margaret remained cooped up together inside the house for the duration. Margaret was completely miserable. Not only was the company bad, but also their confinement in a closed-up house occurred during the hottest part of summer. By each afternoon, the house was sweltering. On more than one occasion, Margaret pumped water into a bucket, went upstairs, undressed, and sponged herself off. It was the only way to get cool. She would lay atop the bed listening to the buzzing animals and wishing with all her heart that she could truly be Missus Russell Chadwick.

She so desperately wanted to be his wife. Even though he was moody, he wasn't entirely disagreeable. Russell was smart and attractive. He provided for her every basic need. He was God-fearing, and seldom swore and never drank. And he was congenial to everyone he knew. "*All except for me,*" she thought sadly. "*He acts so differently around me than he does with everyone else.*" But, Margaret knew she could have done a lot worse. *But why doesn't he want me? It doesn't make sense.*

Relief came on the sixth day. Around mid-morning, all the locusts suddenly flew away. Margaret went with Russell to survey the damage. The beautiful acres of corn and wheat were gone. The vegetable garden was gone too. It seemed as though the locusts had destroyed everything edible. Margaret was nearly brought to tears by the loss. She wanted to reach out to Russell, to support him, but feared his rejection. She would not risk it again. "I'm so sorry," she spoke simply.

Speechless, Russell headed toward the barn. The horses and cow, having been cooped up in the barn, were restless and eager to stretch their legs. The pigs and hens were quite content, having gorged over the last few days. When Russell walked over to the grain bin and peered inside, he let out a sigh of relief. Yet again, he was grateful to see that the insects had not touched his feed supply for the animals. It had been a real challenge these last five days, getting out to the barn amid the hopping and flying bugs. But he had gone in and out of the doors as fast as possible in an attempt to keep the barn grasshopper free. Of course, a few had gotten in through some cracks, but thankfully, only a few. However, this feed supply was limited and would not last through the winter.

Russell fidgeted with his newly grown beard while Margaret comforted the horses. "Guess I'll be going into town today if you want to come along," he said soberly.

Margaret's eyes brightened. It would be wonderful to get out. "I'd love to go," she answered with her best smile.

An hour later, they were on their way. Margaret had changed into her brown dress and wore the straw hat atop her head. She had some of her saved money to spend in her little bag because she planned to treat herself to something nice in the general store. Her mind spun with possibilities.

Out of character, Russell began a conversation. "I want to wire my brother first to tell him not to come for harvest. There's nothing to harvest and I'd hate for him to make the trip for nothing."

"But don't you have to clear the fields?" Margaret asked.

"Yes, but there's no rush. When we leave the telegraph office, I need to order feed for the animals so they can eat this winter. Our corn and grain would have helped feed us all. Let me know how much I should order to feed us through the winter."

Margaret frowned. Oh dear… She thought about it carefully. "How many months are we talking about?"

"September through April, at least. After then, we can get crops from the south."

After more general conversation, Mister and Misses Chadwick arrived in town. It was bustling with activity. As promised, they stopped first at the telegraph office. Margaret talked with acquaintances outside while her husband went in. Together, they walked toward the store. Along the way, they spoke to several friends. Russell and Margaret were both dismayed to learn that very few other farms in the immediate area had been harmed by the locusts. Theirs seemed to be the worst hit.

"It just doesn't make sense," she later said to Russell after their friends left.

He shook his head in disbelief. "I know. I can't understand it at all."

Still shaking his head, they entered the store.

"Hi, Chadwick," Fred, the clerk called out. "Be with you in just a moment." He continued to help a woman with her child.

Russell walked over to the counter and began to flip through the pages of a mail-order catalog. Margaret walked over to the yard goods. She had it in her mind to make herself a cool dress, one with short sleeves that she could wear around the house. She fingered bolts of material. There was fine linen and cotton, some flannel and wool for making winter clothes, and even a few satins and silks for formal occasions. She had no need for those. Margaret pulled out several items from the shelves and placed them in a pile on a cutting table. She also gathered ribbon, thread, lace and buttons.

Russell ambled over. "What are you going to make?" he asked curiously.

She smiled sweetly. "Some new clothes for myself. I'm tired of working in these hot dresses."

He pointed to the flannel and wool on the table. "Then what are those for?"

"Winter clothes, of course. I know it must get cold here and I want to be prepared. Winters were always cold in Cincinnati," she explained.

Russell only nodded. Before either of them could speak again, Fred walked over. "What can I do for you folks?"

"We need supplies," Russell answered. "Lots."

Grinning at the thought of a big sale, Fred led the couple over to a counter. He pulled out a ledger book and a pencil. "I'm ready," he told them.

Russell began to call out the items they would need for winter. He had it all memorized in his head. "Wheat, corn, oats and hay for the animals," he began.

Fred stopped writing. "What do you need all this for? Don't you already have it?"

"Afraid not. Had a swarm of locusts come down and eat it all," he answered humbly. "We'll need everything, including food for us too, but Margaret's in charge of that." He nodded in her direction confidently.

Margaret felt genuinely appreciated. Almost grimacing at the large list, she began, "Peas, beans, tomatoes, onions, potatoes, squash, pumpkins, cucumbers, cabbage and carrots for canning. Berries too if you can get some. And we're running short on tea, coffee, flour and sugar."

Fred wrote down all the items and smiled. "You two are going to keep me in business for a while. Thanks! Is that all you need?"

Margaret pointed to the material on the table. "I need some cloth too."

"My wife handles that department. Let me get her for you," Fred offered. He walked into the back room which connected the store to their second floor living quarters. He hollered out, "Deborah, Margaret Chadwick is here and she needs your help with the yard goods." He returned to the store and smiled at the waiting couple. "She will be with you in just a moment."

"Thank you," Margaret told him, stifling a grin. Most people didn't just go around yelling for each other from across a room, much less from one floor to another. She wandered around while she waited. Russell and Fred were gathering some of the needed supplies when she spotted a roll of screening resting against a far wall. She walked over to it and touched the fine wire mesh. Since they were the only ones in the store, Margaret decided to be a little playful too. She raised her voice and called out, "Russell, come see this."

His head popped over a sack of grain. She motioned for him to come and see. He set down the heavy load and walked over. "What is it?"

"Screening. Can we get some for the windows? It would be so nice to have a breeze through the house but not the bugs. Plus, if we had had it earlier this week, it would not have been so dreadfully hot inside," she reasoned.

Russell scratched his mustache, as he did most times that he was thinking about a subject. "Very well," he nodded. "Get it."

"How much do you think?" Margaret asked.

Russell reached for the roll. "Let me handle it. Fred and I will figure it out. He propped the big roll on end. "Hey Fred, we'll be needing some of this too."

Deborah appeared from the back room. "Sorry it took so long, Margaret. I was putting the baby down to sleep."

"That's fine. I found something else I wanted in the meantime," Margaret confessed.

"So, you need yard goods?" the woman asked.

Margaret looked over Deborah's shoulder at her pile of bolted material. "I need some yard goods cut, but I'm not sure how much I will need."

"Come with me," Deborah said, leading the younger wife over to the table. She had her suspicions that Margaret needed some loose fitting clothing to accommodate a new baby. How exciting!

When the women were at the table, Deborah whispered, "Are you going to have a baby?"

Margaret flushed in astonishment. "No," she replied with embarrassment. "I just need some cooler dresses for working around the house and a few warmer ones for winter."

Deborah was visibly disappointed. Russell and Margaret were the cutest couple in town. Their babies were going to be precious. "Oh, I'm so sorry," she apologized. "I'll just get these cut for you."

Margaret touched the heavy tan wool. "Deb, please give me double length of this one. I think I'll make Russ a coat for Christmas."

"That's a fine idea," the lady answered, hoping to smooth over her impertinence.

Quite some time later, Russell and Margaret were heading home with their wagon almost completely full of supplies. Margaret was glad that the preacher's wife had taught her how to can food. She would be canning for the next several weeks, considering how much food they had now.

"I'll make some frames for that screen. Should take me only a week to get them all done," Russell spoke suddenly.

"That's fine, Russell. I appreciate you getting that screen. I think it will really improve the house."

He nodded. "I think so, too. They will be nice to have."

Just then, they heard horse hooves galloping wildly behind them. Someone was shouting too. Husband and wife turned around. Russell's eyes popped open wide in surprise.

"Henry!" he shouted, nearly standing up in the moving wagon. He pulled the reins to a quick stop as the horses whinnied in protest.

Margaret watched as a young man galloped alongside them. He was grinning from ear to ear. "I see you took my advice, big brother," he teased.

"How are you, Henry? What are you doing here?" Russell asked, shaking his brother's hand in greeting.

"I read about the locusts in the area. Thought I would come out and help you if they came by," he stated.

"Thanks, but you're too late," Russell returned with a hint of sarcasm.

Henry's face fell. "Oh no. Did they do much damage?"

"It's all gone. Destroyed everything. I have nothing to send to Father," the elder brother replied.

Henry shook his head slightly. "I suppose that's a risk you'll take every year. Say Russell, are you going to introduce me to your pretty lady?"

"Oh, sure. Henry, this is Margaret, my wife."

"Your wife!" Henry repeated in a loud voice. "You dog! Why didn't you tell anyone? Mother will be crushed, and thrilled. You are going to be in so much trouble!" Henry then tipped his homburg hat. "How do you do, Margaret? I'm Henry, Russell's little brother."

Margaret smiled at the young man. He looked similar to Russell, only his hair was darker. He was dressed quite well too. He certainly was no farmer. "Glad to meet you, Henry," she returned politely.

"Russ, how long have you two been married, so I can tell mother when I get back?"

"Two months."

Henry shook his head. "You're bad, brother, real bad. But you found a right beauty for a wife," he added with a wink toward Margaret.

Margaret felt herself blushing furiously. She liked Russell's younger brother already. She wondered how old he was. "Henry, how long will you be staying with us?" she decided to ask. She silently wondered where he would sleep. There were only two bedrooms in the house.

"As long as it takes, I guess. Russell, I'll help you clear out your fields. Maybe we can salvage some of the crops," he suggested.

"There's no use trying that. Nothing is left."

The brothers chatted easily for the remainder of the trip home. Margaret listened eagerly as Henry informed Russell of the rest of the family. Margaret learned that both his parents were eager to hear news of their eldest son. Russell had three brothers. Henry was eighteen and the next in line. The other two were much younger. Their father owned a food market.

"Mother sent you a birthday present," Henry stated.

"She did? I guess it is time for my birthday. I hadn't even realized it," Russell confessed.

Margaret turned to him, "When is your birthday?"

"August thirty-first."

Margaret wondered what he would think when he found out she was older than he was. But at the rate they were going, he never would. The thought made her grin.

Henry had a strange look on his face. "You mean you didn't know?" he asked Margaret.

Innocent, she shook her head. "No. He never told me. I've found out more about Russell from you in the last fifteen minutes than I have with him for the last two months," she teased truthfully.

Henry thought this very odd, but kept his mouth shut. He wasn't one to go prying into other people's business. It didn't sound like his brother to be so unspoken though. Usually, Russ was very outgoing.

When they finally reached home, Russell assisted Margaret from the wagon. "Once we unload, I'll go show Henry the fields," he said out loud. He then leaned down and whispered into her ear, "Move all your things into my room while we're gone. We can let Henry stay in the guest room for his visit."

Margaret was shocked. Was he serious? Did he finally plan to share his room? It was too much after all this time. She stared, wide-eyed for several seconds. At last, she nodded.

Henry placed his bag on the front porch so he could help unload the wagon. "You've made quite a change with this place in the last four months," he told his brother.

Russell nodded toward his wife. "Margaret did it all really." Honestly, he was proud of the way she took care of things.

"Impressive," Henry stated. "Margaret, well done. My brother is lucky to have you."

Margaret nodded and smiled. Henry sure was good for her ego. "Let's have steak tonight for supper," she suggested as a treat for their guest. "Russ, will you cut us some meat from the smokehouse?"

Russell lifted a sack of corn, "Sounds good to me."

The men finished unloading and Russell brought in the requested meat. After they left for the fields, Margaret hurried upstairs to move her belongings. She first took in the four dresses, then unloaded the two drawers containing her personal undergarments and nightgown. She gulped at the thought of Russell seeing her in a nightgown for the first time. She wished it were prettier because it was only plain white linen. If only it had lace or ribbons… Oh well. Too late to think of that now. She gathered what few toiletries she owned and placed them on Russell's desk. While there, she just happened to notice some papers stacked on top. The first one read 'Marriage License' across the top. Excited to read it, she did.

Margaret could not believe her eyes. The groom was listed as Russell Chadwick, but the bride's name was not her own. It was another lady named Ethel Peabody. Who in the world? Margaret looked at the document more closely. It was dated February fourteenth, but was unsigned at the bottom. Margaret was both angry and confused at the same time. She left the paper on the desk so Russell would suspect nothing.

Saddened by the discovery, she mindlessly prepared supper. All of her thoughts centered around Ethel Peabody. Who was she? Where was she? What happened to her? Did Russell love her? Maybe she was the reason their marriage was so casual. Margaret determined to find out all she could on Ethel Peabody. In the back of her mind, Margaret was convinced that Ethel was a prettier, smarter, wealthier woman. It gnawed at her confidence relentlessly.

When the men returned, the table was laid out with hot steak, warm bread with honey and butter, baked potatoes and fresh peas.

Cold lemonade filled a nearby pitcher. The house now smelled of baking apple pie.

"Margaret, you're amazing!" Henry exclaimed. "You did all this in two hours?"

In order to avoid crying, she kept her gaze away from Russell. She concentrated on making Henry feel welcome in their home. She forced out her best smile. "Thank you, Henry. I did all this and prepared your room," she bragged playfully. "Can I pour you a lemonade?"

Both men removed their hats. "That would be great. I need to wash up before I sit down at your pretty table though. Which room is mine?"

Margaret pointed upward as Russell answered, "Up the stairs to the left."

Russell stood at the bottom of the stairwell, waiting for Margaret to look at him. Purposely, she turned her back to him and finished work in the kitchen.

"I'll just go wash up too," he spoke, to get her talking.

Margaret remained quiet, closing her eyes against the sad thoughts which hurt her heart so deeply.

Henry came down first. "My mother will be so eager to meet you, Margaret," he said happily. "When I tell her she finally has a daughter, she will jump with joy."

"I'm eager to meet her too. I've never had a mother," she answered.

"You haven't? Why not?"

They both heard Russell's footsteps coming down the stairs. Margaret waited until he was in the room before answering Henry's question.

"My mother died soon after giving birth to me," she explained. "And my father left me when I was eight. I haven't had a parent for a long time."

Russell furrowed his brows. "Your father left you?"

She decided to clarify. "Actually, he left me at an orphanage when he went off to fight the war. He never came back for me."

"That's terrible," Henry consoled. "Well, Mother and Father will be pleased to have you as one of their own." He silently wondered why Russell had not known this information.

Russell said grace and the three began to eat the fine meal. Margaret spent all her energy talking with the amiable Henry. They laughed and chatted easily. Henry shared amusing stories about Russell's childhood and delighted her with information about their parents. When the meal was over, Margaret asked, "Would either of you care for apple pie? I can make coffee too, if you like."

"I'd like some, but no coffee," Russell replied.

Henry rubbed his full stomach. "That meal was so good, but I think I can make a little more room for apple pie if it is as good as the dinner. No coffee for me either."

While Margaret worked near the stove, Henry asked his brother, "When is Margaret's birthday? Mother will want to know."

Russell looked at Henry blankly. He had no idea. "I don't know. Margaret, when is it?"

Henry realized now that something strange was going on. His brother should know this information. Apparently, he did not know much at all about his plucky red-haired wife.

"October thirteenth," she answered, placing a pie slice on a plate.

Henry eyed his brother and his wife suspiciously. They were congenial toward one another, but certainly did not act like a young couple in love. Margaret was avoiding eye contact too. Henry ate his pie with a mind full of curious thoughts.

After supper, the men sat on the porch watching the river. Margaret worked at the kitchen table, cutting out a new dress from the light green cloth. They obviously forgot that she could hear their conversation through the open window.

"Brother, I'm glad you took my advice to find another wife. Quite frankly, I like Margaret more than I ever liked Ethel," Henry admitted.

Russell stared off into the damaged fields. "How is she?"

"Forget about her. You have Margaret now."

"That's right, I have Margaret now," Russell murmured without emotion. "But I still love Ethel. Now tell me how she is!"

Henry was annoyed by his brother's shallowness. If he still loved Ethel, then why did he marry Margaret? It didn't make any sense. "She's expecting a baby, due sometime this winter," he finally said.

Margaret's broken heart pounded. Was it Russell's baby? She gulped and put a hand on her now churning stomach. She wanted to cry out and scream. She wanted to beat her fists against him and yell at him for trapping her in a loveless marriage. How could he crush her heart like this? He was so cruel!

Russell stood and walked to the top step of the porch. He kicked his boot against the rail and walked away toward the barn. Henry wondered what was going through his brother's head. Obviously he was not yet over losing his first fiancé. Henry heard a sniff inside the house and realized their entire conversation was overheard. He felt terrible, and decided to go inside.

Margaret sat on a chair next to the table. Her hands covered crying eyes.

"Margaret?" he called out almost apologetically.

She sniffed and looked up.

"Did you hear us talking?"

She nodded, looking at him with eyes as red as her hair.

Henry knelt down before his heart-broken sister-in-law. "I'm sorry, Margaret. I shouldn't have opened my big mouth. Please forgive me."

Margaret placed a hand on his shoulder. "I'm not angry with you, Henry. It's your brother who has hurt me. More than you can know," she sobbed. "Is it his baby that Ethel carries?"

Henry bit his lip. "I don't think so. Russell never told me that they…" he stopped himself before saying too much, but he knew that Margaret understood.

"Who is she?" Margaret asked, wiping her eyes with her dress sleeve.

"She is the girl that Russell was going to marry last winter. She never showed up on their wedding day. We found out later that she ran off with someone else and married him instead. She lives in Chicago now," he explained.

Margaret cried a little bit more, but Henry continued to explain. "After she left, he was suffering so much. I know that his heart was broken. When he told me he was leaving town to start a new life, I suggested that he find a new love too. That's why I was so happy to see him with you this afternoon. I thought he had gotten over Ethel and fallen in love with you. I must admit Margaret, I truly don't understand what is going on."

"I don't either, Henry. But thank you for telling me about her. It explains a lot," she told him sadly. Margaret stood and slowly began to gather her sewing. "I don't feel well, Henry. Please excuse me. I think I will go to bed now."

"I'm so sorry," Henry said again.

Margaret managed a weak smile, piled her things on the kitchen counter, and went upstairs.

Henry watched as the pretty red-head went up. His brother was a fool! Margaret was a much better woman than Ethel could ever dream to be. A sight healthier too, in more ways than one. She had a nice full figure and a pretty face. And that red hair! She had a heart too, which was more than he could say for Ethel.

Henry grew more and more angry at his brother as he sat there. Why would Russell get married when he obviously loved another? Well, he was going to find out. With determination, Henry stormed out to find his brother.

"Russ?" he called out. He found him in the barn sitting on a bale of hay. He seemed melancholy. "Tell me something. How come you got married to Margaret?"

Russell looked at his younger brother as one might look at a fly hovering over their dinner plate. Why did he care? He shrugged. "To get you and everyone else off my back," he finally barked.

"Why would you go and do a fool thing like that?" Henry asked in disgust.

Russell was silent for a few minutes before speaking. "To protect myself," he finally argued. "I never want my heart shot to bits again. I sent off for her, you know. She's a mail order bride, someone no one else wanted. I did her a favor, giving her a nice home. She takes care of me and the house and that's all I ask. She works hard and never complains, which is exactly what I wanted."

Henry shook his head. "You are pathetic, brother. Your wife is inside right now crying her eyes out because she heard what you said on the porch. You may not get your heart broken again, but hers is. Wake up, brother. She is a great wife and you don't deserve her!" he yelled angrily. Henry then turned and stormed away.

It was late when Russell emerged from the barn. The house was dark and silent. Russell decided to sleep in the parlor. There was no use disturbing Margaret if she was asleep in bed.

Morning came too early for Russell. He tossed and turned during the night, dreaming about Ethel and broken dreams. Henry came down as the parlor clock struck six. He seemed a bit more refreshed than Russell. Margaret was nowhere to be seen. Usually, she was the first one awake.

"Looks like we're on our own for breakfast," Russell announced. "I'll make some coffee and bacon."

Margaret slept soundly through the morning. She had cried much during the night and finally fallen into a hard sleep around three. Before she slept though, she considered her options. She could stay and try to make it work with Russell or she could go back to the agency and ask them to find her another husband. After all, the marriage had not been consummated; she could easily have it annulled. Before falling asleep, she had decided to ask Susan for advice. She was her most trusted friend.

When Margaret finally came downstairs at eleven, the men were working in the fields. She could see where they had begun to level the destroyed crops. Margaret placed a sheet of paper on the table which she had taken from Russell's desk. She hastily left a note telling him she would be at the Grady's house for the afternoon. She would return sometime after supper.

Since both horses were in the field, Margaret would have to walk the five miles into town. This would have been a good day to have a cooler dress. She sighed and began the walk. It took quite a while, but she finally made it. Luckily, some friends from church had offered her a ride the last mile. When she reached the house, Margaret was hot and dusty. Thank goodness for the shady bonnet that she'd made out of extra blue calico. It was trimmed in lace and a bit fancier than the curtains of her home.

"Margaret! What brings you here?" Susan asked. She looked tired and held her back as if it was stiff.

"May I talk with you?" Margaret asked, nearly in tears again.

"Come in, come in." Susan looked worried. Her friend did not look good.

Susan poured Margaret a cold glass of water and sat her down on the parlor sofa. Reverend Grady came in, but Susan shooed him away with her fingers.

"I need your advice, Susan. You're my best friend, and I don't know who else to go to. Will you help me?" Margaret asked weakly.

"I will certainly try," she said, feeling sorry for her friend's obvious distress. Susan tried to ignore the pain in her back as Margaret began to tell her story.

The new wife explained the entire situation holding back no detail about her so-called marriage to Russell Chadwick. Margaret wept when she told her friend what Russell had said the night before on the porch. "What should I do, Susan? What should I do? He doesn't love me. I need love. Or at least have someone who cares about me."

Susan held Margaret's hand. "He cares about you more than he knows, Margaret," she began. "When you said your vows here, did you mean what you said?"

Margaret nodded. "I did, at the time. But I assumed he would at least try to like me and keep his promises too."

Susan furrowed her brows. "I think you should give him a little more time. Stay and try to make it work, at least a while longer."

Margaret wiped her eyes. She was afraid Susan might say that.

"He will see what a wonderful person you are," Susan continued. "He's a man. They learn slowly. If his heart was broken, it will
take time to heal. Kindness goes a long way. And remember, you
will always be loved by God. He will not forsake you…" Susan took
in a sharp breath and winced.

Margaret noticed her friend's grimace. "Susan, are you in
pain?" For a moment, Margaret forgot her own troubles.

"I don't know. I've been hurting all day. Maybe it's just the
heat," she replied. Then she smiled. "Please stay for a while, regardless."

Margaret looked at her friend's bulbous abdomen. "Susan,
when is your baby supposed to arrive?'

"Any day now actually," the preacher's wife answered with a
little nervous laughter.

"Do you think this could be it?"

Susan cringed. "Honestly, I hope not. I'm so nervous about it.
I've never done this before."

Margaret managed a smile. "Susan, you rest here. I'm going
for the doctor. Who do you use?"

"Simons, but Jack is here. Send him. I want you to stay with
me," the friend requested.

Margaret called for the preacher. Close to panic, Jack left in
a hurry.

"Do you think it's really my time?" Susan asked.

"It sure could be, but I don't know much about this either.
I'm used to taking care of the babies after they come," Margaret
admitted.

"I want to go to my room. Will you help me in there?"

Margaret wrapped Susan's arm around her shoulder and helped
her into bed. After another five minutes, Jack returned with Doctor
Simons. The doctor asked Jack to leave the room for a few minutes.

The doctor smiled and nodded. "It's definitely today, Missus
Grady," he spoke after a quick evaluation. "Your baby will be here
soon in fact."

Margaret was instructed to boil water to sanitize the instruments. Once the baby was born, it would be washed with the sterilized water as well. It would be cool by then of course. Margaret also gathered linens. Jack chewed his fingernails nervously in the parlor.

When Margaret returned to the bedroom, she passed the distraught minister. "Pastor, would you be so kind as to send word to my husband? I am going to be delayed since Susan has asked me to stay and help." Not only would it let Russell know why she would be late, but also give poor Jack something to do. Margaret was actually glad not to have to go home tonight. She was not ready to be face to face with her so-called husband.

Susan's labor lasted all afternoon and partly into the night. At eight thirty-five, the baby boy was born. He was large and healthy for a newborn. Margaret had seen them much smaller.

"Oh Susan, he's beautiful!" she exclaimed. "I'll go tell Reverand Grady." She turned and headed for the door. "Congratulations, you have a fine son," she boasted.

Jack jumped with excitement and pride. "And Susan?" he questioned. " She is well?"

Margaret nodded. "Doing quite well, considering. You can see her in just a few minutes."

The doctor reviewed the baby's health and Susan's condition. He gave them both a good billing. Once the room was tidied up, Margaret invited the Reverend to enter.

"Reverand Grady, you are a lucky man. This is a fine boy and your wife is fit as a fiddle. A bit tired, but a few day's rest and she'll be good as new," the doctor spoke. He shook Jack's hand firmly.

Jack half-listened to what the doctor was saying. His gaze never left the small bundle lying in bed beside his wife. The little boy squirmed, opening and closing his mouth.

Margaret watched with jealousy as Jack walked over to them. He knelt down beside the bed, placing a kiss on Susan's forehead. He placed a second on the baby's head. "You couldn't make me prouder," he said softly. He smiled at his wife with pure, deep affection. "What a lucky man I am!"

Margaret's heart ached for the day she might have a baby too. Would Russell be that happy? If only... No use dreaming about what would probably never happen. She was just not going to get love in this world, nor get the chance to give it to any of her own children. A small tear trickled down her cheek. Her heart was envious, but she was truly happy for her friends.

"You will stay with us tonight, won't you?" Jack asked.

"What?"

"You will stay with us tonight, Margaret, won't you? Please! I don't know anything about small babies, and Susan is in no condition to take care of him. I'd be in your debt if you would stay and help me," he pleaded.

It felt good to be needed. "I'll stay, sir, if you need me," she consented.

"Oh good. Thank you," he sighed with obvious relief.

"Well...I'll be back in the morning to check on everybody," the doctor said.

"I'll show you out. Thanks so much..." Jack was saying as they walked toward the door.

Margaret looked at Susan, who wearily smiled down at her baby's face.

"What will you name him?" Margaret asked curiously.

"Jack Junior," she replied smiling. "J.J. for short. Won't that be cute?"

"Would you like to rest now, Susan? What can I do for you?

"I think I will try to feed him first. Would you be willing to bring me some food? I know I could never sleep with this empty stomach. It will help me regain my strength too," she decided.

"Very well." Margaret left to gather the food. She made herself and Jack a meal too while she was there. None of them had eaten in over eight hours. All three ate informally in the bedroom. It seemed almost scandalous to host a dinner party in such a location. But no one really seemed to mind. They devoured the fried chicken, lima beans and mashed potatoes. Afterward, everyone agreed to get some rest while they could. Margaret slept on the sofa. She did not awake again until morning. Not hearing any noise from within the bedroom, she decided to make a hearty breakfast.

Once the eggs and sausage began to sizzle in the skillet and the aroma from a pot of coffee wafted through the house, Jack emerged from the room.

"Good morning, Missus Chadwick," he greeted cheerfully.

She smiled at him. "You sure are cheerful. Good morning to you too," she returned. "How are Susan and J.J.?"

"Sleeping right now. They were up a few hours ago. She fed him and they both fell back to sleep," he replied with a yawn. Jack then took a deep breath to wake up. "Mmmm, that smells great. You're going to fatten up that skinny husband of yours before too long," he teased.

Margaret had to admit that Russell had filled out slightly in the last two months. And to her surprise, she had actually lost a little weight. "I take that as a compliment."

"It was, undoubtedly," he returned. "If you don't mind getting out the plates, I'll go get some fresh milk from the cow."

She nodded her approval. When he returned several minutes later, Margaret asked, "Should I make Susan a plate?"

He set down the bucket of milk. "Let me go see if she's still asleep. I'll be right back."

Margaret served his and her plates while he was away.

"She says you had better make her a plate, and a big one too!" he said with a grin.

Margaret readily complied. She handed Jack the loaded plate after he grabbed his own from the counter. "She wants you to come and join us again too," he added.

"I'm a third person. Are you sure? I feel like I'm imposing…"

"You are not imposing, and Susan is insisting that you stay. Apparently, you give her more courage than I do," he winked.

"Well, if you say so," Margaret replied. "Just let me pour us all some drinks and I'll join you."

Margaret spent most of the day with the couple and their new baby. Several friends dropped by with food and gifts. It was a very happy occasion and she was thrilled to be part of it. She acted as hostess for the entire day since Susan was unable to leave the bed.

"Tomorrow," Susan promised. "I'll be good as new."

As the sun was setting over the far horizon, Margaret decided it was time to go home. She had to face Russell, whether she wanted to or not. She bid farewell and promised to return in a few days. As she gathered her hat, someone else knocked on the door.

"Oh honestly," she mumbled with aggravation. "Can't you people stop coming for one minute so I can go home?"

She opened the door to find Russell staring at her face. "Hi," he spoke in a friendly voice. "Is the baby born?"

She was speechless. "Uh, yes. It was born last night," she finally managed to say.

"Well, can I see it?" he questioned.

She dropped her hand from the doorknob and looked at the rug on the floor. "Sure."

Margaret led the way to the room and announced the new visitor. Susan and Jack eagerly ushered him in.

"Come see my son," Jack bellowed proudly.

Russell looked at the small child. "Doesn't look anything like you, lucky kid," he joked with his friend.

Susan looked at Margaret with a twinkle in her eyes. She had hoped Russell would come for his wife if she stayed away long enough. All was not lost for her new friend.

"Russell, you would be proud of Margaret. She took excellent care of us all," Susan complimented.

"Glad to hear it. She takes good care of me too," he admitted freely

Jack slapped Russell on the shoulder. "So, when are you two going to have one of these things?" he teased. "Margaret will make a fine mother. She knows how to take care of new babies. Showed me all kinds of stuff today."

Margaret returned her gaze to the floor. She would not get upset thinking about what he had said. The day had been too good to let it go to waste now.

"Oh, I don't know, Jack," was Russell's reply.

After brief chit-chat, Russell made his excuse to leave. "Well, I'm sure you must be tired, Missus Grady. I'll go and let you rest now." He turned to Margaret. "Would you like to come home now?" he asked.

"I was about to leave when you arrived," she admitted.

He nodded. "Good. I'll drive you."

After farewells to the new parents, the young couple left. Margaret decided to speak very little and give Russell a chance to talk.

Halfway home, he opened his mouth. "I'm sorry you heard what you did the other day. I never intended to hurt you."

She remained silent.

"Anyway, it won't happen again," he admitted.

Margaret wondered if that was all he was going to say. Disgust filled her heart. "Is that all you have to say to me?" she demanded.

"What else do you want me to say?" he wondered densely.

Margaret took an angry deep breath. "How about starting by explaining why you tricked me into marriage? Do you ever intend on making me your wife? Were you listening to the vows the day we got married, Russell? Maybe you need to go back and read them again. You are supposed to love, honor and cherish me. Apparently you do none of the above. You are also supposed to cleave only unto me and we are supposed to become one flesh. Have you forgotten about that too?" she fumed. "When I said those vows, I meant them. I've tried hard to love you. I've taken good care of you and your home and have just been waiting for you to get over what I thought was shyness or gentility by giving us so much time together. But I've had it, Russell! I'm angry and hurt by what you did to me, but I made those vows with you and I plan to honor my part whether you do or not!"

Russell took the verbal lashing quietly.

"Furthermore, if I ever hear that woman's name mentioned again in my presence, you'll be sorry," she warned sternly.

No more words were spoken for the duration. Margaret helped herself down from the wagon and entered the house. She made sure Russell could hear her cheerfully greeting his brother as he unhitched the team.

That night, Margaret dressed in her nightclothes and lay in Russell's bed nervously. Russell had not reacted to her scolding at all and wasn't sure if that was good or bad. She wondered if he would sleep in his room tonight. After a time, the doorknob turned. Margaret practically held her breath. Russell entered quietly. She could tell he was looking in her direction. It was a cloudy night, so no moon shed light on the bed.

"Are you awake?" he whispered.

She determined what to say. "Yes," she finally answered softly.

"I have some extra pillows. I'll make a pallet on the floor and sleep there," he explained.

"You're welcome to sleep here, if you want to share," she offered boldly.

Russell swallowed hard. He just couldn't do it. "Not tonight. We wouldn't sleep well bunched up together," he said, making up the best excuse he could think of.

"Goodnight, Russell," Margaret said unemotionally.

"Goodnight, Margaret."

Things continued in such a manner for over two weeks. They returned to their normal routine, but slept in the same room. Margaret always had the large soft bed, Russell always took the floor. It was dark in the room when Russell entered, and he never saw Margaret in her nightgown. He slipped out early each morning, giving his wife privacy to dress. At least the newlyweds were making progress. He was a little more talkative in the evenings since Henry was there.

One nice Sunday evening in September, they all sat on the porch.

"I think we should go to the church social," Henry said. "Preacher Grady mentioned it today. Did you take note when it was?"

"Next Saturday," Margaret replied. "It's a pre-harvest celebration before everyone gets to work."

"That sounds like fun," Russell agreed. "We should go."

Margaret smiled inwardly. Russell was making an effort, at least. She looked down at the new green dress she was wearing. He had given her a compliment on it earlier today. The bodice was a separate piece from the skirt and fit her perfectly. Actually, it was very flattering with a scoop neckline and short gathered sleeves. Margaret had decided to postpone making the other cool dress. Fall would arrive soon and she would have no need for it. For now, she had to concentrate on making Russell's Christmas gift and her matching warm dress.

"Hey Russ, you got a bathtub around here anywhere?" Henry wondered aloud. "If I'm going to be dancing with the ladies, I sure don't want to smell like a dirt ball."

Margaret and Russell both chuckled. "Yeah, it's in the barn though. We can drag it out and take turns," the older brother suggested.

"What about me? I'm sure not taking a bath in broad daylight!" Margaret huffed.

"Oh, be a sport!" Henry teased. "I won't look, promise."

Margaret swatted at him playfully. Russell smiled at their game, but said nothing.

The following Saturday afternoon, Margaret eagerly heated water on the stove. She would add it to the cool river water Russell had already pumped into the bathing tub. Freshly washed undergarments lay neatly on the kitchen table. She would wear her pretty yellow dress tonight. It would be the first time Russell had seen her in it since the day they got married. Margaret prayed he would show interest in her at the dance. She spied the special soap she had purchased yesterday afternoon at the store. It would be a rare treat to wash out her hair and body with store bought soap.

"Russell, this water is ready if you would haul it out for me, please," she requested through the open window. It was early afternoon and the men were allowing her to bathe first. That gave her more time to finish getting ready. The festivities began at six o'clock with a picnic supper. The contests and dancing came later.

Margaret hoped she would at least place in the apple pie contest. It sat cooling on the kitchen counter this very moment.

Margaret tucked her undergarments beneath her arm before Russell could see them. It didn't matter that he saw them hanging from the clothes-line every week. They were still personal. Russell entered and lifted the heavy pot. Margaret followed him to the barn with her bundles. She watched quietly as he poured in the steaming water.

"Thank you," she spoke kindly. "I should be done in about twenty minutes."

"Take your time," he returned, walking out and closing the door.

Margaret felt funny undressing in the barn. She was glad that all the animals were outside. It would really have made her feel strange to have them watching. She slipped into the tepid water. It was comfortable on this warm day. After submerging herself to her chin, Margaret closed her eyes and relaxed briefly before washing. She remembered the wonderful bath taken at the hotel in Chicago. That had been her best ever.

Margaret washed her face with water before reaching for the soap. She wet and scrubbed her hair vigorously. In the last three months, her baths had come from a pan of water up in the bedroom. Those were hardly comparable to this cleansing. She continued on washing her body down to the dirt beneath her toenails.

Leaning back, Margaret dunked herself once more rinsing away all the soap from her hair. She felt wonderfully clean. After stepping out of the tub, Margaret realized that she had not brought a clean towel with which to dry herself. She wondered what to do and glanced at the clothes she had worn earlier. They were too dusty. She could call for Russell, but he would have to bring them to her. That would be a problem. Margaret briefly considered air drying. But no, that would take forever. "Russell?" she yelled out from a crack in the door. She then stepped into a horse stall for cover.

He came running across the yard. "What's wrong?" he called out.

"I need a towel please. I forgot one."

Russell walked off toward the house and returned half a minute later. "What do you want me to do with it?" he asked.

"Bring it to me, of course!" she shot back with exasperation.

Russell debated what to do. If he went in, he might see her. He did not want to be tempted. He decided to close his eyes and walk in with the towel dangling from his outstretched arm. "Here it is," he spoke loudly.

"Oh honestly, Russell! I'm in the horse stall. You can't see me. Please put it on the milking stool," she instructed.

Timidly, Russell peeked through one eye, making sure she was telling the truth. With relief, he opened the other one and walked more confidently to deliver the linen.

"A body would think you are twelve years old sometimes the way you act so timid. I swear Russell, you are no man sometimes," she goaded him.

Russell's spine stiffened at the mockery. She was questioning his manhood. His own wife! Well, he would not be made fun of. "I'm all man, Margaret!" he defended himself.

She scoffed at him, "I sure wouldn't know it!"

He dropped the towel and turned swiftly to leave the barn. Margaret was glad she had struck a nerve. She was getting tired of playing this silly game. She left the security of the stall and dried her body. She then pulled on clean drawers, a fresh petticoat, and a pretty camisole. She then towel-dried her long hair. Gathering her things, she walked to the barn door and peered out. No men were to be seen. She yelled out a warning anyway.

"I'm coming out. Nobody look," she said. When all was quiet, Margaret made a mad dash for the house and ran upstairs quickly to Russell's room. She sat on the bed, wiping dirt from her feet with the damp towel. Her hair would take a while to dry before she could get dressed. Margaret decided to rest a while. She lay on her stomach across the bed. Turning her head to the left, Margaret positioned her hair over one side, letting it dangle toward the floor. Before long, she was asleep.

Russell allowed his brother to bathe first. He came out of the barn looking like a dandy. His hair was combed back neatly, his brown suit neat and wrinkle free.

Russell let out a mocking whistle. "Don't you look the ladies' man?" he teased.

"A young man has to look his best," he beamed. "Besides, you have a wife already. I need to find one. I just never know when we'll meet, so I must make a good impression."

Russell rolled his eyes and headed toward the barn. He stopped short when he realized his clothes were still upstairs. Disgusted with himself, he turned and entered the house and walked upstairs. The bedroom door was shut so he called out, "Margaret, are you decent?" There was no answer. Maybe she was in the privy, so he opened the door.

Russell sucked in his breath when he saw his wife lying across the bed in her underthings. The clothing hugged her feminine body. He gulped and closed his eyes, trying to maintain his composure. He had never seen her in such a state. Nor had he ever seen her hair completely unbound. Taking gentle steps, he walked over to his desk chair where the night's clothing rested over the back. He pulled them up quietly, but his watch chain slipped, clinking against the wood floor.

Margaret jumped in her sleep at the noise. She lifted her head to find Russell staring at her.

"I…I just came for my clothes," he stammered. "Sorry I woke you."

Margaret blinked and sat up sleepily without realizing her state of undress. She watched as Russell's gaze lowered slowly. Margaret looked down, noticing her camisole. Her first instinct was to cover herself quickly with a hand, but she thought better of it. Why couldn't he see her like this? They were married! And, she had just teased him for his modesty. She didn't want to be a hypocrite.

"I..I'm going to take a bath now," he said quickly. He spun and hurried out.

That was twice today Margaret had sent him scurrying. She grinned at the knowledge. Tonight, she was going to have some fun.

"Are you ready?" Henry said, tapping on the bedroom door.

"Yes, be down in just a minute," Margaret answered.

She had spent the last two hours getting ready. After being roused from her nap, she fixed her hair in one of the latest styles. It was pulled away from her face and fastened at the sides of her head with beautiful clips. The hair which hung down in the back was curled using a heated rod. Margaret was thankful that there was a small furnace in the room. She then laced her corset. It was loose enough to eat a small meal, but tight enough to make her look shapely. Margaret pulled on the new lisle stockings embroidered at the ankle. Next, she slipped on a new pair of shoes. They were fine shoes covered with pale silk and decorated across the toe with tiny glass beads. A small heel fit at the back and a single strap buttoned the shoe over the top of her foot. Margaret admired them on her feet. They were the finest pair she had ever owned and was undoubtedly thankful for her trip into town the day before.

Just before pulling on the yellow gown, Margaret opened her new bottle of perfume. She poured some into a hand and splashed it on her hair. She then put some on her neck and beneath her arms. After fastening the hooks on the front of her dress, she dearly wished that Russell had a looking glass in his room. She would at least be able to see her reflection. Margaret opened the door and descended the stairs. The men were waiting for her in the parlor. When she reached the bottom floor, both their mouths dropped open. She nearly smiled in satisfaction.

"How do I look? There's no mirror up there, so I have no idea," she stated half-truthfully.

Henry's eyebrows lifted half the length of his forehead. "Brother, you've got one mighty good looking wife there! You don't mind if I take a few dances tonight, do you?"

Russell was still too mesmerized by her appearance to speak. He had seen her in that dress before, but now, it looked, different. And her hair was down. She had never worn it down before, or curled like that. He grudgingly admitted to himself that she was a striking woman.

"Say, Russ, come back down to the ground, brother!" Henry joked. "I asked if I could have a few dances with your wife," he repeated his request.

"Uh, oh, yeah, sure…" Russell fought to say. "Are you ready?" he then asked slowly.

"I'm ready. Just let me gather the pie and the food basket. Would one of you please get a blanket in case we have to sit on the ground?" she asked.

Russell complied, meeting them outside. Henry carried the heavy food basket. After situating themselves on the wagon, the group headed for town. Russell chatted easily with his brother. Margaret chatted easily with Henry. Henry spoke to them both. Only Russell and Margaret seemed to have nothing to say to each other. Margaret determined not to worry about her distant husband tonight. She was going to have a good time.

The merriment was underway when they reached the church building. At least fifty people already milled about, talking and laughing. Children ran every which way playing games and squealing. Margaret entered her pie in the contest and found company with Susan. The baby had grown nicely in the past few weeks and everyone was doing well. Susan and the minister were a bit sleep deprived, but other than that, they were thrilled with the new addition to their family.

"I'm so glad things are going well for you," Margaret told her friend.

"Thank you. And how about you? Have things changed any?" Susan asked.

Margaret managed a weak smile. "Not much. But he has begun to offer me more compliments," she confessed. "I'm trying to be patient with him, but I lost my temper this afternoon and scolded him."

Susan patted her on the arm. "Just have faith, dear."

Jack stood on a chair and welcomed everyone to the fall festival. A brief prayer was spoken and the food baskets were opened. Margaret joined her husband and Henry on their blanket. Everyone enjoyed the wide variety of food available at the pot luck dinner. When the meal was over, it was announced that the competitions would begin.

The men could sign up for both arm wrestling and a three-legged race. The children could enter a sack race, and a greased piglet scramble. The women's pie contest was a bit more dignified than the other games. It would be judged last, just before the dancing began.

Henry and Russell jumped at the chance to compete. Both were soon disqualified however from arm wrestling, having only two chances to try before being beaten.

Margaret tried to cheer her husband, "Good try, Russell. Maybe next time you'll beat that Mister Johnson."

He acknowledged her with a nod. After many rounds, the winner was determined and handed a blue ribbon. The crowd cheered for his triumph. Next came the three-legged race. Margaret and Susan, with several other friends, watched merrily as their husbands strapped themselves by the leg to another man. The gun fired and off they went. Margaret held her breath as her lean husband and his brother gained the lead. They held on until just before the finish line when Henry tripped and they both fell face first into the dirt. Margaret tried not to laugh as Russell spit grass chunks from his mouth.

The children's games were quite a sight. Boys and girls of all ages lined up in flour sacks. At the gun fire, they hopped madly toward the finish line. Half of them fell before reaching the end. Some cried in disappointment. Others laughed at themselves. All the winners were given blue ribbons.

The greased pig event was just for boys. A small arena was sectioned off with bales of hay. All the boys stood atop, waiting for the greased piglet to be released. The first boy to hold onto the pig for a count of five seconds would be the winner. While watching the event, Margaret thought she had never laughed so hard in all her life. The boys scrambled wildly trying to attain the prize. She clapped loudly for the young man who finally claimed the ribbon.

The final event was at hand. Twenty-seven pies had been entered in the contest. All the women waited eagerly as a panel of four judges tasted every one. The field was narrowed down to the ten. At least hers was among the finalists. That was an honor in itself.

Susan's husband Jack was one of the judges. Margaret knew he would not be partial, but hoped that he would prefer her pie over the others. Margaret looked around to see if Russell was watching. She spied him and Henry talking to some other men over near the horses. "Oh well," she sighed. Maybe he would pay her some attention later when the dancing began.

"Missus Margaret Chadwick," she heard a man's voice call out. She looked up. The four finalists were being chosen. Margaret jumped slightly in excitement. Hers was in the running. Several friends came over and patted her on the back.

"Good luck," Susan whispered.

Margaret hoped with all her might. She had never won a contest before. Maybe it would impress Russell if she won. Oh, she hoped she did. The judges each took one last bite and wrote down their choice. Everyone drew near to hear the winner.

"In third place, we have Misses Bonnie Merriweather," the university president announced. The crowd cheered and clapped as the elderly lady received her white ribbon.

"The second place red ribbon goes to Miss Anna Simpson," he announced. Anna blushed a nice shade of pink as she accepted her award.

The announcer stalled for time, building anticipation when he said, "Miss Simpson will make a good catch for some lucky young man."

The crowd laughed with delight while Anna turned crimson. Margaret closed her eyes and crossed fingers on both hands.

"Ladies and gentlemen, our final choice for this year's pie baking contest, and winner of the blue ribbon, is Missus Margaret Chadwick," he boomed.

The crowd clapped loudly. Margaret smiled with pride from ear to ear. She tried to be humble, but was very pleased with herself. She walked to the front of the crowd to accept her blue ribbon.

"I'm so happy for you," Susan cheered. She had purposely not entered a pie this year to give her new friend a chance. It was, after all, a variation of one of her recipes that had won.

"Congratulations," Anna Simpson said in a spirit of good sportsmanship.

"Thank you, Anna. Congratulations to you too," Margaret returned. As Anna had done, Margaret pinned her ribbon to the front of her dress. After the crowd disbursed, Margaret searched to tell Russell and Henry her good fortune.

"Margaret?" Anna said timidly, reaching out.

"Yes."

"Would you please introduce me to Russell's brother? I've seen him in church for several weeks, but we've never been introduced," she admitted, blushing again.

Margaret smiled, knowing the young girl must have a crush on him. Anna was thin with long brown hair. Margaret figured she was about seventeen years old. "Sure, Anna. I'd be glad to."

The women linked arms, as women do sometimes for support, and sauntered over to the men. Henry saw them coming first.

"Hey, you won!" he shouted at Margaret. He walked over, giving her a big bear hug. "I knew you would. Your pies are great!" he complimented. "Look Russ, your wife has the blue ribbon."

Russell smiled at Margaret, but remained where he stood. "Congratulations. It's well deserved," he said.

Margaret returned her attention to her brother-in-law. "Henry, I would like to introduce the runner-up, Miss Anna Simpson."

"How do you do?" he said, tipping his hat.

"Hello," she grinned shyly.

"So, you took second place," Henry observed. "Is there any of the winning pie left? I would love to taste it."

Anna delighted in taking him over to the pie table. Margaret and Russell were left alone. "I just can't believe I won," Margaret stated happily as she tried to coax her husband into a friendly conversation.

"That's real good. I'm glad for you," he returned.

Just then a group of three men walked up to them. They were some of Russell's friends. "Hey, Chadwick, we need your opinion on something. Can you come with us?"

He looked at them as if relieved to have a reason to leave. "Sure," he called out. He turned to Margaret. "I'll meet up with you later." He then turned and strode away toward the other men.

Margaret was sorely disappointed. She stood there alone, wishing to God that her husband would pay her some attention. He was being more evasive tonight than he had been in a long time. It felt like he was purposely avoiding her. Margaret didn't know whether to be hurt or angry. Music began to play in the church yard. Margaret noticed several fiddlers, banjo players and other musicians. Not having much else to do, she wandered over to listen to the music, taking her blanket upon which to sit. Susan and Jack joined her on the lawn. Several couples paired up to spin to the lively reel. Hands clapped, feet stomped, voices whooped and cheered. It was a grand time for most participants.

"Susan, let me hold J.J. so you and Jack can dance," Margaret offered.

"Are you sure?"

"Absolutely. I've no one to dance with. Let me hold him so you can have some fun," she said, reaching out her arms.

Susan handed over the sturdy baby boy. Margaret held him snuggly against her warm body.

"Where is Russell anyway?" Jack wondered.

"He went off with friends," the heart-broken wife replied. She waved a hand in his general direction.

The minister and his wife danced a lively step. Henry and Anna bounced around to the music too. They both laughed as though they were having a grand time. Trying not to feel sorry for herself, Margaret concentrated on cooing with the baby. He was a sweet little thing.

Over the next hour, Margaret alternated between holding the tiny Grady baby and dancing with several other partners. Jack asked her twice, as did Henry. So did a few other men. But not Russell. Susan noticed the situation and formulated a plan. She leaned over and whispered something into Jack's ear. Margaret grinned, thinking they were sharing private secrets. Jack stood and waited for the next song to end. He then walked back into the center of the dance area and held up his hands.

"Gentlemen," he announced loudly. "This next dance is ladies choice."

Giggles and squeals filled the air. Some women immediately tagged their desired partners. Others went about it shyly. Some in the crowd disapproved, but since it was suggested by their minister, they said nothing. Margaret watched the women's selections with interest until Susan nudged her on the arm.

"Go get Russell," she encouraged.

"No. He obviously doesn't want to dance with me," she excused.

"Honestly girl, go get him! This is your choice, not his." Susan urged her with a nod.

A small spark flickered in Margaret's head. It would be fun to dance with him, just once tonight. She would do it. "All right, I will," she stated with determination. Margaret stood and scanned the darkened horizon for her husband. She found him not too far away standing under a cluster of trees with several other men. She clenched her fists and walked determined steps in his direction.

"Russell dear?" she called out to get his attention. "This dance is ladies' choice and I pick you."

Russell's expression was unreadable. He gave his friends a last look and walked toward her. The music began. Margaret boldly took him by the hand and led him into the group of dancers. They positioned themselves properly. Her hand was on his shoulder, the other in his palm. His free hand held her on the side of her waist.

Margaret looked into his eyes. It would sure be easier to live this false marriage if he were less attractive. But honestly, those soft green eyes and blond hair with his tan skin and muscular build made him hard to resist for any normal woman. He was a good dancer too, as it turned out.

"You dance well, Russell," she spoke sincerely.

"Thank you, so do you."

"Tonight is my first time actually. I've only danced with children in the past," Margaret admitted.

Russell tried not to look her in the face. It would be more than he could handle. She was so beautiful tonight, but he was trying to do everything possible not to think of it. That was why he had intentionally avoided her. He did not want to be tempted by her lovely smile, her womanly figure, her gentle voice or her delicate scent. He had to be true to the vow he made to himself. He could only be faithful to one woman, and it was still Ethel.

The dance ended all too soon for Margaret. Russell released her, thanked her and returned to his group of friends. Margaret was nearly heart-broken. Sadly, she returned to her spot on the blanket. Susan wanted to reach out to her friend. She could see the hurt and disappointment on Margaret's face. She silently said a prayer for her friend's marriage.

Margaret was thankful when the evening finally ended. She gathered the blanket and loaded it into the wagon. She also retrieved the food basket. She remained quiet during the long dark ride home. Only a lantern swinging form the side of the wagon lit the way. Henry spoke of nothing else except Anna Simpson.

"I am in love, big brother!" he confessed passionately. "I think I'll come back at Christmas time. Would that be all right with you?" he asked without waiting for an answer. "I just hate to leave this week now, but Pa needs me. I have so much to tell them when I get home. Say Margaret, would you mind getting letters to Anna if I sent them to you? She said she would accept them and write to me too. I hope you don't mind…"

Henry continued on in such a manner for the entire ride. Margaret was greatly relieved to know their house was just around the next bend. She needed quiet, calm quiet for her nerves. Russell drove into the yard and pulled the horses to a stop. Margaret did not wait for assistance, and hopped down from her seat quickly. Henry slid off the back and picked up both blanket and basket.

"I'll put these up for you, Margaret. I know you're tired and I won't be able to sleep for hours," he admitted.

"Thank you, Henry. Goodnight," she said as her steps went wearily up the front porch.

Margaret entered Russell's room and closed the door. Her body felt numb as she unfastened her lovely yellow dress. Piece by piece, she removed her clothing and pulled on her nightgown. She was just putting away her other garments when Russell entered the room. He was taken aback for a moment at seeing her in a gown. The light from the lamp behind her lit the silhouette of her body inside the thin cotton garment. Her hair still fell in long cascades down her back. Margaret saw Russell staring at her and turned her back to him. She had nothing nice to say to him at this moment, so held her tongue.

"You could have let me know you weren't in bed yet," he barked softly while pulling off his black boots. "I would have waited until you turned out the lamp."

His comment was the last she could tolerate for the night. Margaret spun around in a fury. "Russell Chadwick, I truly do not care if you see me in my night clothes. I hardly doubt that you would notice me if I walked in front of you stark naked!" she shouted knowing full well that wherever Henry was, he could hear too. "Just what kind of a husband are you to leave me alone the entire night? You are loathsome and certainly no gentleman. You are a dirty, low down skunk and are the poorest excuse for a man I have ever seen!" she finished, placing her hands defiantly on her hips. Margaret's heart was thumping wildly.

Russell clenched his jaw. This was another jibe at his manhood. The woman standing before him was more alluring than he even dared imagine. He would show her what a man he was! He could prove his manhood without sacrificing principles. He walked swiftly to her and grabbed her by the arms. "I'll show you what kind of a man I am!" he growled.

Margaret was shocked when Russell's lips came down hard upon her own. It was the first real kiss they had shared. It was her first, ever! His fists held her upper arms tightly, holding her to him. His mouth was relentless as it sought satisfaction.

Margaret stiffened in fear at first, but then her body betrayed her anger and warmed from his passionate kiss. Her limbs weakened and she began to return his attentions. Russell's kiss became more demanding and more delirious. Margaret's hands reached for his waist, holding him gently at the sides.

Russell's heart was betraying him after all. A yearning and tortured cry escaped from his throat. Realizing that he was being drawn into passion, Russell quickly released Margaret from his grasp. "Don't you ever doubt my manhood again," he warned as he took a step back.

Margaret was stunned. Her body was alive everywhere from his embrace. How could he release her so suddenly? Wasn't it wonderful for him too? She took one step forward. He took one step back. He was toying with her again. Margaret's emotions surfaced once more. "You are cruel, Russell. Cruel!" she shouted before jumping into the bed. Margaret reached over and turned out the light. She buried her face into the pillow and cried. He had made her feel so good, for just a few seconds. Why was he denying her? Denying himself? Margaret remembered the other marriage license. Ethel. For some reason, she had to be the reason. He still loved her. That had to be it. Sobbing anew, Margaret decided that she wasn't sure how much more of this marriage she could take.

When the tears finally stopped, anger returned. She heard Russell tossing and turning on the pallet below. At last, sometime around midnight, he left the room, slamming the door on his way out.

Two days went by and not a word was spoken about that night. Margaret ignored her husband as much as possible, trying to make Henry's last two days with them all the more pleasant. Henry's bags were packed and sitting by the door on the appointed day. Russell, Henry and Margaret all ate a hearty breakfast.

"Henry, I'm sad to see you go. You've been good company these past few weeks," Russell said.

Henry screwed up his face. "Why would you want me around as a third wheel when you have Margaret? Honestly, Russ! If it were me and Anna, I wouldn't want you nearby," he stated.

Margaret chewed slowly as she watched Russell's reaction. He squirmed a bit in his chair, trying to think of something to say. When he remained quiet, Margaret decided to answer for him.

"I'll tell you why he likes you here Henry. It's because he doesn't care for me or my company and with you around, he has a very good excuse to avoid me. In fact, I doubt he would notice if I disappeared," she said angrily, throwing down her napkin. Margaret glared at Russell who sat watching her as though he were amused.

"Henry, it was wonderful meeting you. You are a charming young man. Have a safe journey home and please give my regards to your parents," she said, giving him a warm hug. Then she stuck her nose in the air and turned her back on Russell. "I'm going for a walk." Margaret grabbed her bonnet near the door and left abruptly. She just could not remain in the same room with Russell another moment without screaming. She had tried. Honestly, she had tried to take Susan's advice and stick with him. But her patience was gone. Something had to give. In her misery, she began to pray.

After a few minutes, Henry came running down the road and caught up with his sister-in-law. "What was that all about?" he asked breathlessly. "Russ won't tell me anything."

Margaret was really too angry to cry, so it surprised her when tears began to seep into her eyes. "Oh Henry, why couldn't he have been more like you? I could love him so much then," she admitted.

Henry wrapped his arms around Margaret in comfort. He knew that there was something strange going on between the two newlyweds, but he just did not know what. Russell certainly did act casual around her. It was not his usual self.

"It's not a real marriage," she sobbed. "I don't have a wedding band, and the marriage has never been… never been…" her voice trailed off as she realized she could not say what needed to be spoken.

Henry looked suspicious. "Never been what, Margaret?" he asked softly. When she did not answer, he provided it. "Consummated?"

Margaret nodded and closed her eyes in shame. She felt very awkward at this moment, but Henry needed to know. She valued his opinion as Russell's brother. "Do you think he thinks I'm too ugly? Is that why he hasn't..."

Henry could not believe what he was hearing. It was incredulous. His brother had not yet fulfilled his duties to his wife, three months after their marriage? It did not make sense at all. It was absurd! And Margaret was so very, very lovely, both physically and spiritually.

Henry rubbed her back in small circles. "Margaret, I do not know my brother's reasons, but I think he is a blind fool. You are a wonderful woman, and if you had been my wife, I would not have wasted a second declaring my affections and proving them in the proper manner."

She sniffed. "Really?"

He smiled. "Really."

Margaret was quiet for a moment before saying, "Thank you, Henry. You are a good person."

Henry gave her a swift kiss on the cheek before saying, "You know I would like to stay and help get this resolved, but I just can't miss my train. My parents would wring my neck if I delay one more hour. I promise to come back around Christmas though. I'll send you those letters for Anna."

Margaret nodded.

"Do you want to come back to the house with me?" he asked.

She shook her head. "Not yet. I want to walk a little farther."

He understood. Tipping his hat, Henry turned back toward the house. Margaret knew he needed to fetch his bags and horse and ride into town with only one hour before the train left. In a way, she wished she could return with him. Maybe one day, she would get to meet his parents. Russell's parents. Margaret wondered how two brothers could be so different.

It was at least an hour later before she returned home. When Margaret first stepped into the house, she thought an animal had been inside. Chairs were overturned, food was on the floor, and dishes lay scattered throughout the kitchen. "Russell, are you here? What happened?" she called out. When there was no reply, she searched the entire house. No Russell. Margaret glanced outside toward the privy, but the door hung open. He had to be in the barn. She walked back outside to ask him what on earth had wreaked so much havoc on the house, and created a mess for her to clean.

The barn door was cracked so she walked right in. Her breath caught short in her throat when she spied Russell sitting on some hay and leaning back against the wall. He held a thick cut of steak over one eye. Blood had congealed along his bottom lip.

"What happened?" she asked.

Russell squinted at her through one eye and grunted. "Never you mind," he barked.

Margaret walked closer. "Let me see, Russell."

He made an angry face, but lifted the piece of meat. His eye bulged red and swollen, matching his bottom lip. Margaret covered her mouth. "Oh my! Can I do anything?"

As if it were too painful to speak, Russell answered slowly. "Just leave me alone, please."

Margaret retreated back to the house. She was not sure whether to be happy or sad. Apparently, Henry had gotten the best of his older brother. It made Margaret smile to picture them fighting, over her, of all things. Maybe Henry had put Russell in his place. Maybe he had scolded him and told him he was disgracing the family name. Maybe…

Margaret mulled many thoughts over in her mind during the morning as she cleaned the kitchen. She also returned her belongings to the second bedroom. It would be good to have her privacy again. She was actually looking forward to it. Maybe now they could make a new start. Maybe Russell would learn to love her. But even if he didn't, she had to admit that life here on the farm was still better than her life in Cincinnati. Here, she had her own room in her own house. She had her own garden and some very special friends. Her time was her own too, since she could do as she pleased. By the end of the day, Margaret was actually singing to herself as she prepared the evening meal.

Just at sundown, Russell came in and removed his hat. He looked at her briefly and headed toward the stairs. "I'll wash up before supper," he stated, holding his left rib cage.

Margaret could see a grimace for every step taken. Henry had really beaten him badly.

There was stew for supper. The evenings were actually turning cool now, so the meal was welcoming. When Russell returned, he walked slowly to his chair. The prayer he offered was brief, but thankful. He ate slowly, mostly sipping the broth over his swollen bottom lip. Margaret had actually made the stew on purpose, hoping it would be easy for him to eat. His eye had already turned a nice deep shade of purple.

"Fred's wife, Deborah at the store, told me that the rest of our order would be in the first week of harvest. If you need any help canning, I'll be glad to do it. I'll be sure to get those screens up on the windows too. I know I promised to do it several weeks ago, but Henry was here and..." Russell spoke, cutting his sentence short.

Margaret was pleased that he was offering to actually do something with her. "I would appreciate your help. Some of my friends have promised me yields from their vegetable and herb gardens too, to make up for some of our loss. Some will have to be dried and some canned," she replied.

Russell sat quietly again for a few minutes. "Margaret, when did you say your birthday was?"

She swallowed a mouthful before speaking. "October thirteenth."

He nodded once. "Good. It's still a few weeks away. If you want to have some friends over, we can."

Margaret raised her eyebrow. What was he saying? "You mean, a party?" she questioned.

"Yes," he nodded again. "If you want to have one."

She thought about the concept for a moment. "I've never had a party," she spoke honestly. Deep down, her excitement grew. A slow smile spread on her lips. "Yes, I think that would be very fun. Thank you."

Margaret smiled as she cleared the table. Maybe he would redeem himself slowly. This was a good start. A party, just for herself. How much fun would that be?

The remaining days of September came and went. True to his word, Russell helped Margaret in the kitchen preserving food to last through the winter. They spoke more openly on subjects other than their marriage. It did seem as though Henry's attitude adjustment techniques had worked somewhat. For that, Margaret was thankful. Russell's eye and lip had healed, as did his bruised ribs. Margaret's heart was healing too. She felt herself liking Russell more and more each day, now that he seemed different. He was finally offering her a glimpse of his real self that he so freely gave to everyone else.

He had finally begun to build frames for the window screens too. As soon as his ribs were healed, he had climbed up on a ladder to measure all the windows. He then built the frames. Each window had two frames that would be nailed together once the screen was placed in between. The entire piece then fit nicely on the outside of the glass pane.

"Looks like you're almost done," Margaret said one cool cloudy afternoon in early October. "How many more screens do you have to cut?"

"Just two," he answered, not looking up from his work. Russell wanted to hurry before the rains came. He could smell it on the wind.

Russell had the screen rolled out on the front yard and was cutting it with a knife. The precut sections were piled on top of one another. As he pulled the knife downward, a crack of lightening filled the air. Russell jumped and the knife slipped, just piercing his finger.

Margaret cowered as the bright flash filled the sky. Before the thunder could boom, she was running toward the house. She yelled back at Russell who sat sucking the blood from his cut. "You better come inside before lightening hits you," she warned. "The screens can wait."

Russell stood and walked swiftly toward the house. She was right. The screens weren't worth this. Another crack of lightening sent him running up the front steps. Margaret shivered as a cool breeze blew across the front porch. Autumn was certainly making its presence known. This would probably be the last thunderstorm of the season. And from all appearances, it was going to be a bad one.

"I'm going to get my shawl. Would you like me to make coffee or tea?" she asked.

"Tea would be fine," he replied as he pulled his dirty boots off and dropped them on the porch. Well, he could read his newspaper now. It was going to be an easy afternoon.

Later that night, Margaret lay in bed listening to the rain beat down on the roof. The rains had begun several hours ago and had not let up yet. She and Russell had enjoyed a quiet evening chatting in the parlor about her upcoming birthday party. She had decided on the guest list and wanted to make a cake with coconut, if it could be acquired. She had only had it twice before in a pastry from the bakeshop. The tropical fruit was so sweet.

Margaret had apologized to Russell for forgetting his birthday back in August, but her mind had been occupied with other things.

"Don't worry about it, Margaret," he had said. "I don't deserve any presents."

"All the same, I'll make it up to you at Christmas," she had replied.

Their conversations had gotten much more open. Russell had asked her to bake him a pumpkin pie soon for it was his favorite. He had also begun to ask her more about her likes and dislikes. But still, every night, they never touched and went to sleep in separate rooms.

Another sheet of heavy rain beat upon the window. The winds were picking up too. Margaret could hear it blowing through the trees in the side yard.

All of a sudden, she heard Russell's bedroom door slam open and his heavy footsteps stomping down the stairs in a hurry. Her heart thumped with worry. She jumped out of bed and ran downstairs too. The front door was left wide open. Only a dim light from the remains of the parlor fire lit the room. Even still, Margaret could see the beating wind and rain outside. She ran to the porch and shouted, "Russell, where are you? What's the matter?"

From in the yard, he answered, "Stay inside. I have to get the screens before they all blow awy."

"Can you see them?" she asked loudly.

"Not really," he confessed, searching the ground blindly with his hands.

Margaret ran back inside and lit a lantern. Holding it up, she stepped off the porch and out into the muddy yard. The ground was cold and wet beneath her feet. The rain was almost icy as it soaked her nightgown. "Does this help?" she asked, shining light on the ground.

"Yes, thanks. But you should go back inside."

Margaret shook her head. "You can't hold the lantern and the screens at the same time. I'll help you."

They searched the yard. It took just over a minute to locate the wind strewn sections. Russell placed them securely inside the barn.

"What about the frames?" Margaret questioned excitedly. Her body shivered from the cold and wet as soon as the words were out.

"I'll get them, you stay here for now," he said. Russell ran out into the yard and gathered the wooden squares. When he returned to the barn, Margaret noticed that he too was barefoot and shivering. She yearned for her warm, dry bed.

Russell saw Margaret shaking with cold. Her nightgown was completely soaked and stuck to her body. Her long hair, matted by the rain, hung down to her waist. He turned away quickly, trying not to think of the image before him. In doing so, he spied a horse blanket and had an idea.

"Let's go back under this," he suggested. "It will help keep us warm." After shaking out the woven fabric, he blew out the lantern hanging on a hook and offered his wife one end of the blanket. They huddled together with the cloth draped over their heads. On the count of three, they took off in a mad dash for the house. Before Russell had time to react, Margaret had taken two slippery steps and lost her balance. She landed hard on her bottom in the mud.

"Ahhh," she cried on the way down.

Russell lifted her out of the muck and carried her back to the house in the pouring rain. The blanket was forgotten in the yard. Just as he stepped on the porch, a gust of cold wind whipped across their bodies. Margaret shivered with goose bumps from head to toe.

Russell deposited her gently, just inside the door. Unintentionally, he watched as she stood shivering with the glow of burning embers at her back. Her cotton nightgown was now outlined and semi-transparent. The dull light lit her red hair just enough to make it look like fire. There was a wildness about her that was irresistible. Russell took a few steps closer.

Margaret took a step back. There was a funny look to Russell's eyes. It was one she had never seen before and it frightened her a little.

"Are you hurt?" He asked. "Did you fall hard?"

Margaret took another step back, protecting her backside with nervous hands. "No, I'm fine," she replied. "But I am cold and wet. I'll just go back upstairs now," she said, trying to slink toward the stairwell.

"Don't go yet," he begged quickly.

Margaret looked at him curiously. "Why not?"

Russell stepped even closer. "Because I want to give you this," he said softly as he leaned over and took her arms with his hands. He gently pulled her against his own wet torso. Russell placed his lips securely on hers and wrapped his arms around her back. He held her close, as though she might try to escape.

Margaret could feel the fire growing. He was doing it again, building her up just to let her down. She tried to fight it, to resist, but she was so starved for his touch and desperate for affection. Her own breath came quickly as her body yielded to his. On their own, her limp arms wrapped around his back. Strangely, she was no longer cold.

Margaret's eyes flew open as she felt her body being swept off the floor. She looked at Russell in surprise as he cradled her in his strong arms. "What are you doing?" she asked nervously.

He was already walking toward the stairs as he looked seriously into her eyes. "Something I should have done a long time ago, wife."

Margaret gulped as Russell carried her upstairs to claim her as his own.

A small tear of happiness trickled out of the corner of Margaret's eye. She was happy, so, so happy. At last, after all these long, lonely years, she felt loved. Her husband had finally opened up and allowed himself to feel again. He had held her, loved her, whispered to her and kept her warm. Her heart simply soared with joy that she could finally allow herself to love him now. She had wanted this for so long.

Rolling over, Margaret placed a warm hand on Russell's chest. He must have been almost asleep, for he jumped at the touch. "Russell, for all you've done for me, I love you and thank you for it," she said softly. She then leaned over and placed another sweet, soft kiss on his mouth. It felt delightful to be able to give him such an intimate gesture.

When she returned to the pillow next to his, he replied, "You're welcome."

As it was late into the night, Margaret and Russell drifted off to sleep beneath warm quilts. Both were oblivious to the cold wind blowing savagely outside.

Several weeks passed. The day of Margaret's birthday had arrived. Friends would be coming soon for the party. Margaret wore a new two piece dress made from the tan wool she had purchased several months ago. The fit was remarkable and very flattering. Her hair was pulled into a large pretty bun and wrapped with a ribbon. She actually felt beautiful, but she knew it was all in her attitude anyway. It had everything to do with Russell and the wonderful way he was treating her.

In the last few weeks, he had put her on top of the world. Every night, after a long day, he would sit in the parlor and tell stories so funny that her sides actually hurt from laughing. At night, they kept each other warm in the same bed, like married spouses should. Their closeness and friendship grew with each passing day. Margaret was head over heels in love with her husband. His attitude toward her had changed completely since the night of the storm. He was finally showing her his real self, and he was wonderful.

His smile made her heart melt. His voice made her heart beat faster. If only he would say those three words she so longed to hear, her heart would truly sing. She had confessed her love for him repeatedly, but he never responded in kind.

"Be patient and trust God," she remembered the words of her dear friend Susan. And be patient she would. Russell had come so far these last few weeks. She could wait a while more to hear him say, "I love you."

"Where do you want me to put this?" Russell asked dropping off the bottom step of the stairwell.

"What is it?" Margaret said, not turning to face him. She was too busy icing the coconut cake she had managed to make earlier that day.

"Why don't you turn around and find out," he teased.

Slightly annoyed at having to stop her project with only minutes before the guests arrived, Margaret swung around with one hand on a hip. The other held the icing spoon. She gave him an exasperated look.

Russell held out two small packages and noticed how quickly Margaret's expression changed. "Your presents. Where do you want me to put them?" he asked again.

Margaret set the spoon down and walked over to her husband. She wrapped her arms around his neck and smiled sweetly. "Presents? For me?" she asked in awe. Then she smiled. "Thank you, sweetie."

"Actually, only one of them is from me. The other is from my mother. She sent it last week and I had to keep it a secret from you because I didn't know if you would try to figure out what it is," he declared teasingly.

"I wouldn't have peeked," Margaret defended herself. At least, she didn't think she was the peeking kind. She had never been given many presents before, so there had never been the temptation.

Margaret took the two small boxes from his hand. One had a little weight to it, the other was light as a feather. "You know," she began, "if our friends come and see these sitting out, they might think that they were supposed to bring a gift. Maybe I should open them now."

Russell grinned at her eagerness. "Fine with me!" he answered enthusiastically.

Margaret opened the heavier box. Inside was a beautiful cameo surrounded by the tiniest pearls she had ever seen. The woman on the jewelry was beautifully carved. "Oh Russell, it's gorgeous!" she exclaimed with genuine excitement.

Margaret read the small note inside the box. It was from Missus Chadwick, his mother. The cameo had belonged to Russell's grandmother. She was pleased now to pass it along to her new daughter-in-law. With excited fingers, Margaret pinned it onto the collar of her new dress. "How does it look?" she asked Russell.

He nodded. "Looks nice."

Margaret grabbed the other gift and began to tear off the paper. "Your mother sure was sweet to send me…" her voice trailed off. Margaret was choked up at the sight of the second gift. It was a ring, a wedding ring. Her moist eyes looked up at Russell with a thousand thanks. She could say nothing.

Russell stepped forward. "My brother convinced me, in his own special way, that you deserved to have a ring. Sorry I didn't get you one earlier," he apologized.

In a barely audible whisper, Margaret answered, "Thank you."

Russell took it from the box and gently slid the smooth band of yellow gold onto the proper finger. Margaret's hand shook with nervous excitement. Once it was on her finger, she smiled. "Thank you, Russell. I love you."

He smiled in return. "You're welcome, Margaret."

After sharing a brief kiss, Margaret returned to her cake. It was now hard to concentrate on the icing as her eyes kept returning to the shiny band on her hand. This was definitely the best birthday of her life.

As their friends arrived, Margaret easily played the role of happy hostess. The evening was a grand success. Everyone enjoyed cake and punch, laughter, music and a little dancing. Even Russell asked Margaret to dance a few times. She noticed a far away, mystical look in his eyes. She thought it was just the dreamy happiness that she too was experiencing. Every time she looked at him, he was watching her with that dreamy gaze that seemed to penetrate through her very being. Tonight is the night, she thought. Tonight, he will tell me that he loves me.

After the guests left, the young couple quickly cleaned up the kitchen. Margaret was exhausted, but hoped Russell would take her in his arms as soon as they were upstairs. She glanced at him out of the corner of her eye. He was putting up a plate. Silently, she slid over behind him and wrapped her arms around his body and kissed the back of his neck. He was warm, and smelled of soap. "Let's go upstairs," she whispered.

There was a momentary pause, but then Russell spun around and took her hand.

Just before they both fell asleep, Russell let out a long, slow sigh. "I love you Ethel," he spoke clearly.

Margaret's body froze as his words sunk in. She was no longer almost asleep. "What?" she shouted as she sat up in the bed.

"What?" he had the nerve to ask.

Margaret smacked him on the arm. "You said Ethel!" she seethed with furious anger.

Russell made a noise in his throat as he paused to think.

Margaret scrambled out of the bed as she resisted the urge to pummel him with her fists. "Ethel?" she shouted in a rage. Then her emotions got the best of her. Sobs rose out of her throat in anguish.

Russell sat up and blinked in a stupor. He realized what he had done. His fantasy had escaped. His imagined life with Ethel had finally slipped out. "Margaret…" he began.

"I hate you!" Margaret managed between sobs. "You are cruel. Why did you marry me? Have you been thinking of her these last few weeks?"

Russell hung his head in shame. It was true. He knew he was guilty, but pretending that Margaret was Ethel was so much easier than pining away for his lost beloved. What a fantasy he had created, imagining that it was Ethel who so lovingly wanted his touches. It was Ethel who made his supper every night and took care of their home. He even pretended that it was Ethel who shared such enjoyable nights in the parlor by the fire.

"Why, Russell? Why did you marry me?" she spoke again in a calm, pained voice.

"I needed someone to take care of me," he answered. "And to get everyone off my back about what happened. I wanted them to think I had moved on."

By the quivering tone of his voice, Margaret wondered if he too might be crying. But that would be absurd. "You should have hired a maid," Margaret spoke bitterly. "Will you ever love me?" she dared ask next.

Russell shook his head. "I can't. I love Ethel still."

With these words, Margaret's heart shattered into a million pieces. She wanted to get as far away from this man as she possibly could. Quickly grabbing her clothes, she fled the room. Tears fell freely down her face as she slammed the door of the guest room. Her body then slid limp to the floor as she wailed in anguish. She would never be loved. Russell had sealed her fate with his artificial marriage. For hours, Margaret grieved, crying until her body slipped into an exhausted sleep.

Sometime during the night, she woke shivering. Her body ached everywhere as she crawled beneath the covers. As she lay there, Margaret's mind replayed the awful scene and all the hurtful things Russell had said. "Stop," she told herself gently. "Don't think about it." She did not want to start crying all over again, but it just couldn't be helped. Purposefully, she considered what to do.

A divorce seemed like a very good idea. She could return to Chicago once the paperwork was complete. And then, she could find work, or return to the agency. That thought frightened her. This experience had been so bad. If only she had parents to return to… Then another thought entered her mind. Russell had parents, good ones. Maybe…

The ends of her lips turned up just slightly at the thought. Would they let her in? Would they welcome the daughter-in-law they'd never met? Henry would be there. He was great, like a real brother. He was nice to her. Yes! Margaret grew more and more excited as she considered this idea. "Thank you Lord," she whispered. "For that wonderful idea." With these happy thoughts in her mind, Margaret eventually fell back into a peaceful sleep.

The following morning, Margaret dressed early. She would leave today. She would pack, go into town, send a wire to the Chadwicks, then board a train. Her excitement grew with each moment.

After waiting as long as possible, Margaret entered the room where her husband still slept. She dropped her empty satchel on his desk. He jumped with the startling noise. Ignoring him, Margaret swiftly grabbed her things.

"What are you doing?" he asked groggily.

"I'm leaving you," she replied sharply.

A brief look of alarm crossed his face. Russell sat up in the bed. "Where are you going to go?"

"Never you mind," she replied, feeling like he didn't deserve to know.

"I'm sorry about last night. Please stay," he asked.

Margaret stopped her work and stared at him in disbelief. "If you think I want to stay here with you under this roof for another second, you are a fool!"

"But, what will people think?" he questioned.

"Who cares?" she shot back. "It's God I'm worried about. I'll not be near you when lightning strikes again," she stated as she closed the bag. "There's a bolt with your name on it." With that, she spun on her heels and marched out, slamming the door behind her.

Margaret was in the barn hooking her satchel to the saddle when Russell walked out wearing only his long-johns. He looked silly standing there in his bright red underwear.

"You can go into town later to fetch your horse," she spoke with controlled emotions. "You'll be hearing from me, or from a lawyer. Goodbye, Russell Chadwick." She touched the brim of her hat in a manly gesture and hoisted herself onto the horse. She sat astride, and felt very strong about her decision. Without another word, she tapped the horse and urged the gray beast into a fast trot. Margaret never looked back, but she hoped Russell's mouth was hanging open in surprise.

By noon, Margaret had said goodbye to her best friend Susan and was on the train heading east. She would be in Chicago by nightfall and had sent the Chadwicks a telegraph letting them know about her arrival. Hopefully, they would not be put out by this sudden visit. Margaret said a heartfelt prayer, hoping that her in-laws would accept her without too many questions.

During the ride away from Iowa City, Margaret was both happy and sad. She cried several times remembering the hurt in her heart. She had grown fond of her home, her new life, and even Russell, when he was being good to her. But then she remembered that he had just been pretending. Last night, he had broken her heart. It would take a long time to mend. Maybe his parents would be kind to her. She could only hope.

A child cried from somewhere further back in the train car. Margaret sighed deeply. Her dreams of family were gone now too. This was yet another stab into her heart. After a reasonable time, she would find a job to keep herself busy. If her mind had time to think, it would only recall painful memories. Working with children was what she knew best. Maybe, she could take an exam and be a teacher. That would open a lot of possibilities. It would be worth looking into at least, if she was smart enough to pass the exam. She might even go further west. Wouldn't that be exciting?

Resting her head against the window pane, Margaret wondered about Mister and Missus Chadwick. His mother was forty and named Joanna. She was blond, and had been married at sixteen and a mother by seventeen. Ever since, she had been busy raising her sons. Besides Russell and Henry, there was Daniel and John. Daniel was twelve, and Johnny, as they liked to call him, was nine. Both liked to get into mischief too, according to Henry. Their father, George, spent most days working in his food market.

Margaret could picture their house in her mind. Russell had described it to her one night during one of their wonderful conversations in the parlor. It was a modest two story with four bedrooms upstairs and four rooms downstairs. The front door entered into the parlor. Behind the parlor was the kitchen. Next to the parlor was the office and library. Behind that was the formal dining room. Set in between the kitchen and dining room at the back of the house was the staircase.

This family had no idea how lucky they were to have each other. And how marvelous to grow up together under the same roof. Russell had told her how George, his father, had remained home during the war because the Union Army needed him there to supply the troops with groceries. It made Margaret wonder what her life would have been like had her own father survived.

The journey was uneventful for the most part. At the stop in Davenport, one woman tried to board the train with her pet poodle. With her large body and enormous feathery hat, she had made quite a sight arguing with the conductor about her carry on baggage. In the end, the conductor had won out by promising the dog a hearty meal during his journey in an open crate. The crate would, of course, be in the baggage car.

Before dusk, Margaret could see the lights of Wheaton flickering in the distance. This was her destination, an outlying city of Chicago. She sighed with relief. Now, she just hoped that Russell's family would take her in.

"Are you Margaret?" a female voice asked from the platform.

Margaret looked ahead toward the sound. A blond-haired woman wrapped warmly in a wool cloak smiled at her gently. Two young boys stood on either side. They looked remarkably like their older brothers.

"Missus Chadwick?" Margaret questioned.

The lady smiled broadly. "Yes. I'm Russell's mama. Welcome to Wheaton. Welcome to the family." She rushed forward and gave Margaret a gentle squeeze. When the hug ended, the kind mother asked, "Where's my son?"

Margaret took a breath and tried to act sad. "I'm so sorry, he couldn't come too, ma'am. He wanted to get the hogs butchered before winter. I'm sure he will try to join us as soon as he can. He sends you his best." Actually, part of what Margaret had said was true; Russell was planning on butchering the hogs this week. "I hope you don't mind that I came without him."

"Oh no honey," Joanna replied. "I'm just surprised he let you travel alone. It's not like him… But no matter, I've always wanted a daughter. This will be a real treat for me indeed," she gushed. "And please Margaret, call me Joanna, or Mother, either will do."

Margaret beamed. This woman was too good to be true! "I'd like that, thank you, Mother." Just saying it made her heart skip a beat.

"Boys, this is your brother's wife, Margaret. I expect you to be cordial during her visit," Joanna warned her sons.

Margaret smiled at them in turn. "You must be Daniel and you have to be Johnny."

Johnny smiled impishly. Daniel extended his hand. "How do you do?" he asked politely.

Margaret was genuinely impressed. What wonderful manners! She returned his greeting, then asked of Joanna, "Where is Mister Chadwick, and Henry?"

Her mother-in-law replied, "They went to Chicago for a big meeting. Won't see them again until tomorrow afternoon some time." After speaking, she turned to Daniel. "Take Margaret's bag please, so we can go home. I'm chilled to the bone."

The two women and two boys climbed onto the surrey. Joanna herself held the reins, guiding the horses home. Joanna and Margaret spoke freely on various lighthearted subjects. When the buggy pulled onto a drive, Margaret stopped speaking. It was a private lot, barricaded by a low wall covered with vines. Gas lanters lit the entrance. Every window of the home at the end of the drive shone with light. It was beautiful! Margaret almost wanted to cry at the comfort of the sight. It was a home, with a mother and a father. Something she had never had.

"Are you all right, Margaret dear?" Joanna asked suddenly.

Margaret gulped own the lump in her throat. In a whisper, she answered, "I'm fine." She managed a weak smile. "Your home is just so lovely. More lovely than Russell described to me."

Joanna smiled. "Thank you. We like to call it home. And I hope that you will call it home too."

"I would like that very much," Margaret answered as her heart beat happily. This was a dream come true.

The remainder of the evening was spent eating and relaxing. The party of four got to know one another, sharing information and amusing stories. The boys told her of their favorite things to do.

"I like baseball," Daniel declared. "Have you ever seen a game?"

"No. I'm afraid not. But I would love to see one someday," Margaret admitted honestly. "Maybe I could even try to hit the ball."

Nine year old Johnny laughed at that comment. "Girls can't play baseball," he snickered.

Margaret and Joanna both looked offended. "Why not?" they asked in unison.

After reviewing the looks on both their faces, Johnny withdrew his comment and retired to his room for the evening. Daniel joined him for moral support.

"Maybe one day when the weather is good, we can get out there and try our luck," Joanna stated with a chuckle. "Sure would be fun."

Margaret nodded in agreement and stretched her neck from side to side. It was stiff from the ride on the train.

Joanna noticed Margaret's discomfort. "Why don't we retire early too. You've had a long day of travel."

"If you don't mind, I would love to rest," Margaret admitted.

Joanna led her up the stairwell to a room. Margaret had seen all of the downstairs, but this space was new. Joanna opened a bedroom door. "This is Henry's room, but you can stay here tonight. Tomorrow, we will make other arrangements."

"Thank you, for everything Joanna," Margaret spoke politely. "Goodnight."

Joanna gave her one last hug before going back downstairs to lock up for the evening. Margaret looked about the room. An oil lamp burned on a table next to the bed. Joanna must have had the boys light it earlier. The bed was large and looked wonderfully comfortable. Margaret briefly wondered if her traitorous husband had ever slept in it. Probably, she thought with disdain.

Margaret changed into her warm flannel gown, and after turning down the lamp wick, climbed into bed and fell fast asleep. Sometime during the night, the bed bounced and jostled. Margaret screamed in terror.

"Who's there?" a male voice demanded.

Through her scream, Margaret recognized that it was Henry. She abruptly ended the piercing cry. Once the terror was gone, the situation seemed quite amusing. "It's only me Henry," she replied laughing. "Margaret."

The door flew open. Joanna held a lamp in one hand and a pistol in the other.

"Don't shoot me Ma!" Henry yelled as he jumped backwards.

Joanna looked at her son with relief, then glanced at Margaret. The girl looked all right. "What are you doing home at this hour?" the mother demanded of her son. She lowered the weapon.

"The convention let out a day early, so Father and I decided to come home," he explained.

By this time, Daniel and Johnny were also standing in the doorway. Joanna noticed that they were gawking at Margaret, who sat in bed wearing only a nightgown. Her long red hair tossed wildly about her head.

"Boys, back to bed," she barked. "Your father is home." They scampered away quickly.

Margaret heard the door close downstairs and reached for more covers. Her face turned bright pink as she realized her situation. With the covers now pulled up to her chin, she said, "Maybe I should get dressed."

"Nonsense. You sleep. It's very late," Joanna spoke. "Sorry to have disturbed you, dear."

Henry agreed with his mother. "Yes. Sorry Margaret. I sure didn't expect to find you in my bed. Scared the life out of me too," he laughed. "See you in the morning."

"Where is your father?" Margaret heard Joanna ask as she and Henry walked down the hall. She couldn't hear his answer. Margaret wondered what Henry would think about her visit. He knew there was trouble in the marriage. Hopefully, he would keep it a secret. Margaret certainly did not want Joanna to know the truth. At least not yet.

Apparently Henry held his tongue, for Joanna said nothing the following morning. Margaret held her breath as George Chadwick came down for breakfast. She hoped he approved of her. For some strange reason, his and Joanna's approval was important. He gave her the once over and smiled.

"Good morning, Missus Chadwick," he greeted formally. She was well groomed and had a comely face. And boy, was her hair red! George raised an eyebrow, wondering about her personality. Was she suitable for his son? Joanna had said she was perfectly charming. Well, he would have to see for himself.

Margaret nodded politely. "How do you do, Mister Chadwick?" she returned. He was a bit portly, but the features of a once tall, handsome man remained.

"Very well, thank you. So, tell me how you and Russell met," he said all in one breath.

It seemed Henry had told them very little about her marriage. Margaret answered his question with a hint of shame. He asked several more personal questions. Margaret felt as though she were under a looking glass. The room grew hotter and smaller.

"Stop badgering her!" Joanna ordered from the opposite end of the table. "That's no way to treat our guest. And family at that!" she added. Joanna offered Margaret an apologetic smile. Joanna then turned to her inquiring husband. "Don't you have work to do at the store?"

"I just wanted to know about her," he stated defiantly as though Margaret were not in the room. He gulped down the last of his drink. "Henry, you ready?" he hollered up the stairs.

"Almost," came the muffled reply.

Margaret sat quietly until the two men had left. Shortly thereafter, the boys left for school. Margaret was glad that only Joanna remained for she felt very self-conscious after George's grilling.

Joanna noticed Margaret's mood change. She was perturbed at her husband for such callousness. Joanna sat next to Margaret and put an arm around her shoulder. "Sorry about him dear. He's just a man and doesn't think sometimes before he opens his mouth."

Margaret's heart had been low until Joanna's comment. She smiled slowly. How true was her mother-in-law's wisdom.

"Once you get to know him, he's really loveable. Honest," Joanna promised with a grin.

Margaret trusted Joanna's word. Within two weeks, George was loving on her as if she were his very own flesh and blood. It seemed everyone in the family was in love with the new "sister," as Johnny liked to call her. Margaret told Henry all the latest regarding Anna. His parents too seemed interested in the young girl over which their son was so infatuated. The family got along splendidly. They even played a game of baseball one sunny, cold afternoon. Horse saddles were laid out on the front lawn for bases. All the boys, including George and Henry, were surprised at the women's skills. Even wearing hats, coats, heavy skirts, extra petticoats, gloves and scarves, they were able to hit and run.

One windy afternoon in early November, the men in the family decided to go out riding horses while Joanna and Margaret sipped tea in the parlor.

"I wonder why Russell hasn't written to you yet," Joanna mentioned casually. "You've been here for three weeks, and not one letter."

Margaret nearly choked on her pumpkin biscuit. "I'm sure he is busy," she stated quietly, knowing it was a lame, but honest excuse.

"How many letters have you written to him?" Joanna continued.

Margaret bit her lip. "Well, actually, none. It's just we've been so busy, there just hasn't been time." She tried to laugh it off, but noticed Joanna looked displeased.

"I think we, you," she corrected, "should write to him and invite him to join us for Thanksgiving. It would be a wonderful reason to get together as a family. Don't you think?" she asked.

Nodding, Margaret feigned agreement.

"You can use some of my writing paper if you like. I'll go get it for you," she said, walking off excitedly. When she returned, Joanna stated, "I haven't seen Russell since February. I would love to have all four of my boys under one roof again, even if it is just for a few days."

Margaret humored her mother-in-law and moved to a nearby desk. She wrote out a letter, leaving out anything personal. Margaret hoped Russell would decline. His mother would surely put them together in the same room, and that would be dreadful.

All of a sudden, Joanna exclaimed, "Say! I have an idea. Let's go to town first thing tomorrow and post it. We can do a little shopping while we are there. I could use a new dress for the occasion. What do you say?"

It was difficult not to get caught up in her enthusiasm. "That would be fine," Margaret replied. It would be fun to browse the stores.

After helping Joanna prepare a hearty breakfast of baked apples, sausage and flapjacks, Margaret sat down to eat. She was actually excited for today's shopping excursion.

"Joanna and I wanted to give you this," George said, handing her an envelope. "Call it a wedding present if you want, but it's all yours to do with as you please."

Margaret looked at them both curiously before opening the paper. It was money! One hundred dollars to be exact. "Oh! I can't take all this," she exclaimed.

"Our feelings would be hurt if you refuse," George stated, giving her a hug. "You can buy yourself some pretty new duds today, if you like."

As her husband mentioned this, Joanna thought about Margaret's clothing. She only had two plain blue work dresses, one simple brown dress, and the tan two piece dress. Joanna wondered if her husband had noticed Margaret's meager wardrobe. Certainly her son should have provided for a more adequate trousseau. Yes, today, she would make sure that her daughter-in-law had appropriate clothing for a woman of her standing. None of them were abundantly rich, but they were certainly well-to-do.

After the boys left for school, George and Henry escorted the women into town in the family surrey. It was a frigid, gray day.

Everyone was wrapped in warm coats. Margaret had to borrow an extra one from Joanna. All she had was a wool cloak.

"Looks like we might get snow today," Henry said to Margaret as they sat in the back seat. "If it falls heavy, maybe we can all go sledding after church this coming Sunday. Have you ever done that?"

"Not since I was a little girl," she answered. "My father used to take me before the war."

Everyone's mood sobered a bit at the mention of her father. Margaret had told them the sad story of his apparent death and her childhood in the orphanage. Joanna and George had made an extra effort after that to be a mother and father to their daughter-in-law. And it was not hard, for she was a charming woman.

The men dropped the women off near the clothing stores before continuing to their food store. It was arranged for them to return to the same spot at three o'clock in the afternoon. That gave the women six hours to shop. Margaret could not imagine needing that long. It was unheard of. But Joanna took Margaret to her favorite dress shop and showed her off to the head woman. "She's come to visit a while and we need to get her several new dresses. What colors do you think would blend well with her striking red hair?" Joanna asked.

Olga was a tall blond-haired woman with a thick accent. "Hello Joanna, good to see you again. How do you do, Margaret? I am Olga. Let's go to the back room and look over color samples. I'm sure we can find several that are flattering."

The tall woman led the way to a comfortable parlor decorated in hues of orange. It was a lively room, and very feminine. Joanna and Margaret were offered hot tea and crumpets for refreshment. "Please, have a seat. I will return in a moment."

Margaret sipped the warming drink. The ride into town had chilled her more than she had realized. Joanna drank eagerly too. Margaret wondered if her cheeks were as rosy as her mother-in-law's.

Olga returned with an armload of supplies. First, she opened a leather satchel, exposing many wonderful color swatches. "These are the fabrics we have on hand. Margaret, if you have a color in mind that you would like and don't see it here, we can order it from one of the larger stores in Chicago or New York," she explained taking a seat. Next, Olga pointed to the book on her lap. "This book contains dress styles to choose from. Once you pick the dress and the material, we go to the trim room, where you can chose lace, beads, or otherwise to decorate your new fashions."

Margaret was a bit overwhelmed. In her mind, she decided it was easier to go buy a dress already made. But, it would hurt Joanna's feelings if she said so. Taking a deep breath, Margaret began to review her options.

After three hours of deliberation, the choices had been made. At Joanna's insistence, Margaret had ordered four dresses. One was a black gown made from thick, heavy silk. The skirt puffed out in the back and swept the floor with fancy pleats. It was decorated with lace and beads and could be worn to a dinner party or other fancy occasion. The second was a splendid deep purple gown trimmed with black lace. The combination was very striking. The front half of the skirt boasted three ruffles. The back half bunched up and out in volumes of folds. Margaret realized that with all these dresses, she would have to wear her corset and the pillow which fit over her lower back to help the dress fit properly.

The third dress came in several pieces. First was the underskirt, made from a dark green and blue plaid. Along the bottom was a thick green fringe. Next came a simple dress that buttoned from the neck to slightly below the waist. It was made from heavy blue silk. A fitted bodice jacket was the last piece of the ensemble. It was made from the same plaid material as the underskirt. Its large buttons were covered with green velvet, as were the cuffs and collar.

The final dress would be made from a reddish-orange colored velvet. It would be trimmed with cream colored braid. The front of the dress came down to just below the knee, exposing a pleated cream colored satin underskirt. It too, would be a beautiful creation to wear. Margaret could hardly believe all these dresses were for her.

Joanna ordered a two-piece dress for herself in a deep mustard colored silk. Embroidery in matching thread would complete the outfit. "Now where?" Joanna asked as the women left the store. "Oh, I almost forgot the letter. We have to mail the letter."

Margaret had hoped she would forget. Alas, she had not. "It's right here," she said, patting a small drawstring bag.

"Let's go to the post office before getting lunch. Are you hungry, dear?" Joanna asked.

Margaret nodded, but listened as Joanna continued to rattle on and on during the cold walk to the post office. After delivering the letter, Margaret was eager to enter a warm building. The restaurant smelled of roasted beef and freshly baked bread. After taking a seat near the fire, the two women ordered and began to discuss the day's purchases. "We still need to get you a few things," Joanna stated. "I want you to pick out at least two new pairs of shoes and some stockings. Also, you need a heavy coat, and a fur muff wouldn't hurt you either. We can just go down the street to Tanner's store and see what he has."

"I really don't need…" Margaret began.

"Hogwash! You do! I can see that Russell failed to give you a trousseau, so I'm seeing to it that you get one."

"A what?" Margaret questioned.

"A trousseau. Haven't you ever heard of that?' Joanna asked, truly amazed.

Margaret shook her head.

Joanna shook hers in pity. Then explained, "It is a wardrobe that women get when they get married. It's a French word."

"Oh."

By three o'clock in the afternoon, both women, burdened with packages, awaited their ride. "Where are those men?" Joanna complained. "It is blustery cold out here! I know if Russell were here, he would be on time."

Margaret remained quiet. He was a punctual man, but she was in no mood to give him compliments. Joanna was right about the weather though. It was freezing!

Finally, the buggy came rolling around the corner. George and Henry looked pleased with themselves.

"It's about time you two showed up," Joanna scolded. "Margaret and I were about to freeze to death."

Margaret noticed Henry and George exchange a snickering glance. They must be laughing about Joanna's whining. Henry jumped down and helped them load their parcels.

"Looks like you bought out the entire store, dear. Did you two ladies have fun?" George asked as Joanna took the seat next to him.

Her anger was soon forgotten. "We did," she said with a wide smile. "Margaret will pop Russell's eyes out when he sees her next. We had the best time."

"I'm sure you will want to tell us all about it," Henry said in a kidding manner.

And she did too. Joanna described every dress in detail during the ride home. She then told the men about every item purchased at Tanner's store. Margaret knew the men were anxious to get home. She actually felt sorry for them having to listen to mundane details. When George set the ponies at a faster pace, she had to smile.

Within two weeks, no word had come from Russell. His parents were both more than annoyed. "That boy!" George exclaimed one afternoon. "He had better get himself here for the holiday."

"I just can't imagine why he has not responded," Joanna said sullenly. She seemed visibly hurt by her son's silence. "Have you any idea, Margaret?" she asked at last while taking a moment to pause from the task of peeling potatoes.

Biting her bottom lip, Margaret shook her head. "I'm sure I don't know."

"Well, he needs to be here," George mumbled from the table. In a louder voice, he hollered into the parlor. "Say Henry? Aren't you going to town tomorrow to post a letter to that Miss Simpson?"

"Yes Pa," Henry answered. As he looked up from his newspaper, his father walked into the room.

"I want you to do something for me," George said. His voice then trailed off as he spoke to his son.

Margaret wished she could hear their conversation, but it would be blatantly obvious if she stopped rolling out the pie crust and walked into the next room. She hoped George wasn't going to do what she thought he was going to do. Henry would probably be instructed to send Russell a telegram and wait for a reply. Honestly, why couldn't life just stay like it was for a little while longer? She was so happy in this home. Both Joanna and George adored her, as did her brothers-in-law. They had fun together too.

Sure enough, Henry sent the telegram the next morning and returned home with a response. Russell had apologized for not sending a post earlier, but he made the excuse of being terribly busy around the farm preparing for winter. He would, of course, be joining them for Thanksgiving. He would arrive on Wednesday and return home the following Saturday. Margaret rolled her eyes. At least it would only be for a few days.

8

"Hello, everyone!" Russell greeted them gaily as he stepped off the train. He was more dashing than ever with a top hat and stylish cape.

Margaret held back on the platform, allowing her husband to embrace his mother first. Joanna was more than eager to see her eldest son. Margaret felt more self-conscious than ever. After these next few days, Joanna and George would surely know the secret that Henry had kept. It would be obvious by his behavior that Russell was not in love with his wife.

He tossled the hair of his younger brothers, then spied her at the back of the assembly. "My dear," he exclaimed. Russell walked to her in a rush. "You look simply wonderful."

Margaret was shocked. Russell wrapped his arms around her in a big hug and kissed her right on the mouth in front of everyone. Her heart pounded so hard, she thought it would burst. How could this man be so mean and cruel one day, and dashing and charming the next? She did not trust him still.

"Glad you came home son," George said, patting Russell on the back. "We've gotten to know Margaret well these last few weeks. She's charming, simply charming. You did good for yourself, Russ."

Russell smiled at his father. "Thank you, Pa. I think so too."

Henry gave Margaret a knowing glance. He felt sorry for his brother, and for Margaret too. His brother was a fool who didn't know how good he had it. Poor Margaret, her heart would be torn up again after Russell's holiday charade.

"Let's go home," Joanna stated as a brisk wind blew across the platform.

Russell grabbed his bag and they all walked toward the buggy. "We will have to pile in," George said with a grin. "Mother, if our family keeps growing like this, we will have to purchase a bigger carriage," he teased.

Margaret blushed to the tips of her ears. Luckily, they were hidden underneath a warm bonnet. Neither George nor Joanna had mentioned grandchildren since she arrived. Maybe now, with their son here, they felt comfortable broaching the subject. Margaret prayed they would not ask her a question directly. She would surely not know how to answer.

Russell caught the hidden meaning in his father's statement. He decided to change the subject by twisting his words around. "Yeah, Henry. When are you and Miss Simpson going to get hitched? She's been pining away for you since you left. Every Sunday without fail she asks about you after church."

"Russell!" Henry scolded his older brother. "I'll thank you to stick to your own business."

"Now really Henry, there's no need for that. I would like to know too if you are truly serious about this Anna girl," Joanna stated with great interest.

Russell grinned wickedly at his brother. Henry scowled in return. "In fact, she gave me a letter to give to you, but if you want me to stick to my own business, then I guess I will just return it to her on Sunday. I'll let her know she can mail it, if she likes," Russell teased.

Margaret watched as Russell continued to taunt his brother. It seemed everyone joined in the fun of asking Henry about his intentions. When the family finally reached home, Henry demanded the letter.

"Can you at least wait for me to get settled?" Russell asked.

"No. You've harassed me long enough. Now give it here!" he demanded with an outstretched hand.

Russell reached into his pocket and passed off the letter. Henry quickly retreated to his room. Margaret wondered how long indeed it would be before Henry asked Anna Simpson to be his wife. Margaret then hung her new coat on a peg by the door. Her new purple and black dress rustled gently as she walked into the parlor.

Russell let out a low whistle. "You look good, Margaret. That is a new dress, isn't it?" he complimented. "I take it my mother took you shopping?" He gave his mother a quick wink.

Margaret felt more self-conscious now. He was putting on an act and she felt like a display in a store window. Luckily, Joanna changed the subject and barraged her son with a hundred questions. Margaret was more than happy to sit quietly. Daniel and Johnny had a hundred questions for their big brother too. It was late in the evening when the family's curiosity finally seemed to be satisfied.

"I guess we had better turn in for the night," George suggested. "It's so good to have you home."

"Yes, so good to have the family back together," Joanna agreed as she kissed her eldest goodnight.

Russell turned to his wife. "What room are we in?"

Margaret gulped. "Daniel's."

"I assume that is my old room?" he said, turning to his mother.

She nodded. After that first disastrous night in Henry's room, Joanna had put Margaret in Daniel's room. It had a large bed. Until now, Margaret had not known that it used to be Russell's room.

"Shall we?" Russell asked, offering an arm to escort his wife upstairs. He then turned to his parents. "Goodnight all." Russell glanced at Henry who looked rather dazed; apparently, Anna's letter had had a strange effect on him. He had only half listened to the conversations all night. He was definitely distracted.

George and Joanna grinned as they waved goodnight. Margaret knew what was going through their minds. They were thinking that the young couple would rekindle four weeks of missed romance. How wrong they were!

Once inside his old room though, Russell took Margaret by the hand. "Forgive me, Margaret. I can't tell you how sorry I am. I was wrong. Please, let me try to start over," he nearly begged.

Margaret opened her mouth to speak, but he cut her short.

"Please, let me finish. I've spent these last few weeks doing a lot of thinking and soul searching. I know I was wrong to you. I know I hurt you. I didn't write to you because it is hard for a man to admit he was wrong. I was wrong about loving Ethel, but you've got to understand that I was so very much in love with her. She broke my heart when she left me at the altar on our wedding day. I've hardly been myself since. In a hasty decision, I sent away for a bride that I wouldn't have to love. That way my heart would never be wounded again. I was expecting an ugly older woman who wouldn't expect much except food and a roof over her head. Imagine my surprise when you showed up, all young and healthy and pretty in your yellow dress. I tried my best not to get close, but you break down a man's resolve. You were...tempting, but my heart still belonged to Ethel. I was so torn. I know now that she and I were only a dream that I created in my mind. I have to move on but I need your help. Please forgive me. When I saw you at the station earlier all dressed up like a fine lady, I knew I had to beg your forgiveness. I will try to be a better husband; I do know better. It may take me a while to get it right," he concluded.

Margaret stared at his earnest expression as she considered an answer. How could she believe him? He had deceived her before. She pursed her lips. "I want to believe you, Russell, but I do not trust you. It would be nice to start over, but I don't want to have my heart crushed again either. Let's just see how the week goes, and then we will see. I can't make you any promises right now."

Russell nodded. "Fair enough. Want me to sleep downstairs?"

She shook her head slightly. "No, you don't have to do that, but do stay on your side of the bed."

Thanksgiving was a happy day for the entire Chadwick household. Margaret and Russell exchanged pleasant conversation amidst everyone else's excited chatter. The boys were happy to be out of school. Joanna was thrilled to have everyone under one roof. George salivated over all the food on the table. Henry grinned from ear to ear. He noticed the new kindness his brother was showing to Margaret. He wanted them to share what he had with Anna, a true love. Little did everyone know that in the letter she had sent, she had agreed to become his wife. Henry was about to burst at the seams to share his grand news, but wanted to savor the secret privately for just a little while longer.

After games in the parlor all morning, the family enjoyed a wonderful roasted goose with all the trimmings. Joanna and Margaret had done most of the work the day before, so were able to join in the fun activities with the family.

Joanna wore her new mustard colored dress, and Margaret the velvet one with the birthday cameo fastened at her throat. Russell could hardly keep his eyes off her. Several times, she caught him staring and blushed.

"When I go home Saturday, you will come with me, won't you?" Russell finally asked quietly during the main meal.

He had been surprisingly kind over the last few days. He had been the Russell that he normally was to everyone else, the funny, outgoing man with a good heart. Margaret took a deep breath. "Do you promise to keep being yourself? This nice man who is pleasant to be around?" she questioned.

"I do."

"All right. I'll come back."

When Joanna found out that Margaret was leaving, she was actually sad. Of course, she had known it was inevitable, Margaret belonged with her husband. But Joanna had so enjoyed having a daughter to dote on; she had secretly hoped that Margaret might stay. "Can't you move back home?" Joanna asked her son.

"Ma, you know I have a farm to care for. Besides, Margaret and I need our space for a while. Our privacy."

Joanna frowned. "Well, you will come to visit again at least, won't you?"

"Of course we will," Margaret answered. "I was very happy here with you, more than you could ever know."

Joanna smiled and hugged her daughter-in-law.

"You and Father should come to the farm in the spring," Russell announced. "The boys would love to run and play in the fields. There is so much room to roam and we have several big trees in the yard that are great for climbing." As he said this, his brothers began to grin from ear to ear.

"Don't give them any ideas," Joanna scolded . "But you know we would love to come."

"When is a good time?" George asked.

"Sometime before planting, if you just want to relax. But if you want to work, May would be an excellent month," Russell replied playfully.

The younger boys groaned. "Please Pa, let's go in early April," Daniel begged.

Everyone had a laugh over Daniel's humor. Toward the end of dessert, Henry finally spoke up. "You know, we could all go to Iowa before the spring, if we wanted to. Maybe for Christmas," he suggested.

"That might be fun," Joanna agreed. "Is there room in your house, Russell?"

"What would we do all day besides freeze?" George teased. "No. No. A city Christmas is much more fun…"

Henry cleared his throat before his brother or anyone else could speak. "Well, actually, there is plenty to do. Mom could visit with her first daughter-in-law, and meet her second one."

"What?" a round of surprised voices echoed.

"Henry?" Joanna questioned.

"What are you saying, little brother?" Russell asked.

Henry sat back and savored the moment smugly. "You see everyone… I asked Anna Simpson to marry me."

Joanna covered her opened mouth as her eyes bulged. Margaret's mouth popped open too. "Really?" she then gulped in excitement. "What did she say?"

Henry gave her an exasperated look. "Yes, of course!"

Cries of delight came from Joanna's mouth. George grinned with pride. His boys were doing well for themselves and his family was entering a new phase. He was very pleased with his expanding family. Before long, there would be grandchildren bouncing all over the parlor. How wonderful! He would have to purchase another buggy for sure.

Daniel and Johnny seemed only half interested. Girls were of little interest to them, unless they were good at games. It was lucky for Margaret that she was one of the best.

"When will you marry?" Joanna asked, wiping a small tear of joy from the corner of her eye.

Henry answered, "I have to ask her father first, but she and I would like to be married Christmas Day." He turned to Russell and Margaret. "If Father can spare me for a week, would you mind terribly if I came and stayed with you for a few days? I need to ask her father's permission and get other things squared away. Then I would come back here until the wedding."

"Fine with me," Russell answered, looking first at his brother but then at his wife. She was nodding as well.

"How exciting for Anna," Margaret smiled. "I can't wait to talk with her."

"Tomorrow I will go and buy her a ring," Henry told the group. "Anyone want to help me?"

"I'm sure we all will," his mother replied.

"Not me!" Johnny said, rolling his eyes. All this talk of women and weddings was enough to make a lad sick.

"I need to buy a trunk at the store as well," Margaret confessed. "For all my new clothes."

"I need to look around too," Russell admitted. Then with a wink, he added, "Christmas is right around the corner."

So it was agreed that the entire family, with the exception of Daniel and Johnny, would go into town the next day for a fun shopping trip.

Fierce wind whipped around the tracks two days later as the Chadwick family waited inside the terminal for the westbound train. It would reach Davenport by afternoon, Iowa City just after dark. Margaret had mixed emotions about leaving. It would be so hard to say goodbye to Joanna and George. They had been so good to her. At least Henry was coming too; he was always fun to have around. But on the other hand, it would be nice to return home to start over with Russell. He was a new man these last few days. She sure hoped and prayed that it would last.

The incoming train's whistle shattered the hum of voices inside the building. Several small children jumped with fright. Some even began to cry. Margaret gathered the skirts of her pretty new green and blue plaid dress. Russell draped her brown and black coat open so that she could slip it over her arms. After fastening each closure, she grabbed her mink muff. It would surely keep her hands warm.

"Goodbye Russell, journey safely," George said as he shook his son's hand.

"Thank you Father, for everything. For taking good care of Margaret before I arrived," he said.

Joanna hugged them all, saving Margaret for last because her embrace was the longest. A little tear trickled down the woman's cheek. "I'm not good with farewells," she admitted, half laughing at herself.

"We will see you soon," Margaret answered. Anna Simpson's father was a reasonable man. Margaret had no doubt that he would approve of the marriage.

"Bye boys," Russell said to his younger brothers. "When you come to Iowa City, I promise to take you sledding on the biggest hill around." Both boys grinned with excitement.

"Don't worry about rushing back right away Henry," George spoke. "The business will take care of itself while you're away. It's time Daniel started learning the trade too. It will give him a chance to get started after school," he concluded placing a confident hand on Daniel's shoulder.

The trio waved as they boarded the train. Margaret took her seat, reminiscing about the holiday. It had truly been the best month and holiday of her life. There were so many new things to be thankful for, she hardly knew where to begin. Just thinking about this new change in Russell would give her plenty to think about during the day's journey. No doubt they would share a room again once they reached home. The next few weeks were going to be very interesting, possibly even exciting.

After church services the next day, a very nervous Henry walked over to where Anna Simpson and her parents were standing. He wanted desperately to take Anna in his arms, but knew that was not the thing to do at this particular moment. He gulped. "Excuse me, Mister Simpson? May I have a word with you, sir?" he managed.

"Hello, Henry. Back from Chicago so soon? I thought you weren't coming back until Christmas, as least that's what my daughter told me," the man explained.

"Yes, sir. Those were my original plans. But something has come up that requires my attention. May I speak with you privately?" he asked again.

Missus Simpson held a little grin at the corner of her mouth. She had noticed how her daughter had not taken her eyes off of the handsome young man since his arrival at the service. She had her suspicions of what was going on. "Mister Chadwick, we would be pleased if you would come to the house for dinner today. You and my husband can talk as long as you like. I'm sure Anna would like to catch you up on all the news as well."

Henry turned his attentions to the petite woman. "I would be honored ma'am," he answered with a slight bow.

"Very well," Anna's bearded father answered at last. "See you around two."

Russell nodded his head again giving Anna one last long glance before walking out of the vestibule. His heart was pounding so hard he thought he could actually see it throbbing through his coat.

"Well, what did he say?" Russell questioned nosily when his brother returned to the wagon.

"I'm having dinner with them today at two," he replied with slight frustration. He had wanted an answer now.

"That's good. A man is always happier when his stomach is full," Margaret declared teasingly.

Henry gave her a sour look as he pulled on warm gloves. "I'm nervous enough without your jokes, Margaret."

Margaret feigned remorse. "I'm sorry, Henry. I don't mean to tease. But Mister Simpson is a good man. I'm sure he will say yes. You have nothing to worry about."

\

"He said yes!" Henry shouted later that night as he walked in the door.

Margaret put on an I-told-you-so face.

"Congratulations!" Russell spoke as he jumped up to shake his brother's hand.

He and Margaret both sat down in the parlor to listen to Henry's entire story.

"We ate supper first," he explained. "It was good too, and Anna cooked it. Then after the meal, Mister Simpson and I stayed at the table while Anna and her mother cleaned the dishes. I told her pa about my intentions and about the family back home. I made sure he knew I could take care of his girl. He gave me his blessing and let me tell Anna in private. It was wonderful! I just can't believe it."

"So you will take her back home?" Margaret wondered aloud.

"Yes. Her mother isn't too happy about that, but Anna is thrilled. She wants to live near the big city. In fact, she wanted me to ask you if you would help her make a wedding dress. She saw your pretty new dress in church today and thought it was beautiful. Oh, I can hardly wait to give her nice new things," Henry almost sang with happiness.

"I would be glad to help. I will go see her tomorrow," Margaret answered with a smile. It was fun to see Henry so excited about his future bride. With a little twinge of jealousy, Margaret wondered if this was how Russell had reacted when Ethel first accepted his proposal. It was something she would never know.

"It will be a simple wedding, with Reverend Grady presiding. They don't have much money. Maybe I should help Anna buy her wedding dress," Henry spoke as the thoughts went through his head.

"Oh Henry, let that be part of my gift," Margaret responded sincerely. "I have some money saved up. It will be a good way to spend it."

And so it was done. The next day, Margaret went to the Simpson's home. It was decided that she and Anna would visit the dressmaker in town. And, with her help, fashion a gown fit for a future Chadwick bride. Margaret would be paying for all the fabric, lace and notions as part of her gift. Anna had only to pay for the seamstress' time.

"Thank you Margaret," Anna gushed as they hugged goodbye. "I will enjoy having you for a sister."

Margaret was struck silent for a moment. She had not considered the fact that she would have a sister. It was only the brothers-in-law that were a reality at present. Then she smiled. "I will like it too, Anna. I've never had a sister."

Anna giggled. "Me either." Then she waved. "See you tomorrow morning. And please tell Henry I will see him tonight."

Margaret nodded as she climbed into her wagon. Much to Russell and Henry's exasperation, she had insisted on taking the wagon alone to the Simpson house. It was hard for Henry to stay away, but at least he had been invited back for supper that night. With a flip of the reins, Margaret was on her way.

Several weeks passed. Henry returned to Wheaton in search of a home for his new bride. Anna however had assured him she would not mind living with his family for a while. She had never lived in a house full of people. "It might be fun to have such a large family," she had said. Margaret knew just what she meant. Indeed she had grown up in barracks with fifty other children, but it wasn't the same as a mother and father and siblings. And Joanna was a wonderful mother.

As promised, Margaret helped Anna with her wedding dress. The front was covered with embroidery and beads. The actual fabric was a creamy satin. The back billowed out with yards and yards of folded cloth. The train gracefully swept the floor for several feet. Anna felt like a princess in such splendor. Margaret was a bit jealous of the wedding gown, but was still very happy for her friend.

In her spare time, Margaret prepared her home for company. Russell's family would arrive in just a few days. Mister and Missus Chadwick would be staying at a hotel in town, but the boys would be staying at the farm. It would be a good holiday for all of them since the parents would have some privacy and the boys would be able to run wild without their mother watching. Henry and Anna would be staying at a hotel too, but not the same one as his parents. Henry wanted to make sure that he and his new bride had plenty of privacy too.

With the Chadwick's arriving on the twenty-third, Henry would have one full day to finalize plans. Margaret planned a full supper for everyone on Christmas Eve. Anna and her parents were invited too so they could socialize with their future in-laws before the wedding. Margaret had a savory meal planned with baked ham, vegetables, rolls and a plum pudding dessert.

Late in the afternoon on the twenty-third, Russell and Margaret put on their warmest clothing and rode into town. The train would arrive shortly, which was good because there was a light dusting of snow on the ground with more expected soon. Everyone hoped to avoid an early blizzard that would ruin wedding plans. When Margaret and Russell arrived at the station, Anna and her parents were there too.

"I didn't expect to see you today," Margaret exclaimed as she gave a hug to her friend.

"I just couldn't wait until tomorrow," Anna blushed. Then she whispered, "I don't think my parents could wait either."

Both friends enjoyed a secretive smile before turning attentions to her parents. Russell stood chatting easily with them. "I

sure hope this weather holds out a few more days. Sure would hate
to see a blizzard on Christmas Day."

"Just don't seem like God would do that to us," the senior
man said, scratching an old war wound on his thigh. "Dang this
scar though! It bothers me fierce when the weather is about to turn
bad. Just two days, that's all we need. Just two days…" he repeated.

Anna's petite mother turned to Margaret. "I tell you dear,
Anna is sure excited about moving to Wheaton. And her dress is
so beautiful. Thank you for helping her with it."

Margaret smiled. "It was my pleasure, ma'am. Russell's mother
took me to a dress shop in Chicago and we spent half a day picking
out four dresses. Once you choose the pattern and material, the rest
is just fun and easy." Margaret turned to Anna. "You know Anna,
I bet Joanna does the same for you too. She is so wonderful. You
will just love her."

Russell heard these words and felt full of pride for his wife.
He gently placed an arm around her waist. She had turned out to
be quite a fine woman. Not only was she uniquely beautiful, but
also gracious and kind. One seldom found those traits together in
a woman, at least that had been his experience. She was good to
him too and cared for him with all her heart. If only… No. Russell
stopped his thoughts. He would not go there again.

The train's whistle could be heard a mile down the track. Everyone's excitement grew as they lined up to greet the travelers.

"I'm so nervous," Anna confessed to them all.

"I bet Henry is too," her mother assured her.

Margaret and Russell stood together as the great machine
pulled alongside the wooden platform. They strained to find their
family among the passengers still inside the car. Finally, they began
to step down.

"There they are!" Russell shouted over the growing noise of
the crowd. Of course, they were at the far end.

Fighting the onslaught of people, the Chadwicks and Simpons
made their way together. At last they met. Henry walked ahead of
his parents to find Anna. She looked so very pretty in her warm

light blue bonnet and dark blue wool coat. He wanted to reach out and hug her, but wouldn't dare with everyone watching.

"Hello everyone," he greeted instead with a large smile. "Anna," he spoke with a nod of his head. "Mister and Missus Simpson."

"Hello Henry," Anna replied with considerable self-restraint. Her skin was crawling to touch him.

When the rest of the family caught up, introductions were made. George noticed that most of the women were shivering from the cold.

"Why don't we all go to the hotel for supper? My treat. We don't want these pretty ladies freezing on us," he stated.

The Chadwick men gathered the luggage, five large bags in all, and headed down the steps. Everyone else followed.

"I had no idea Iowa City was so large," Joanna observed. "I thought it was a small town," she added as her eyes caught sight of an enormous building further up the street.

"Actually, it's quite populated, Ma," Russell responded. "We have a university and several large buildings, including the old state capital. But it's nothing like Chicago," he admitted.

"How far to the hotel?" Joanna wondered out loud.

"Only a few more blocks ma'am," Anna answered politely.

"Oh please, call me Joanna," the woman requested. "What a sweet young thing you are too. A lovely girl."

"Her father and I are proud of her," Missus Simpson spoke boldly. "But we sure wish she wasn't moving so far away."

"Oh, but it's not that far," Joanna declared as she began a lengthy conversation about how Henry and Anna could come to visit or how Anna's parents should come stay with them in Wheaton. A trip to Chicago would be very exciting. "And we could all go to the opera together," she finished.

"Really?" Anna gasped with eyes lit with excitement.

"Well, we don't have the best seats in the house, but we do have seats, and manage to get there at least once a year," Joanna admitted. "They have wonderful plays too, and several concerts each season."

"Yeah, and it's really, really boring," Johnny added. Daniel concurred with a vigorous nod of his head.

"Someday you will appreciate my taking you boys. You will meet a fine woman like young Anna here who will want you to take her to a concert. And won't she think you are special when you do?" their mother said.

The boys both rolled their eyes but decided to remain silent.

When the group arrived at the hotel, Henry was allowed to remain with Anna while Russell and the boys helped their father take all the bags upstairs. Not long after, the party of ten was seated at a long table near a window. All of them were glad to be out of the cold and wind. Once orders were taken, conversations began.

"Anna, do you like to play baseball?" Johnny asked. This was very important information.

"How about sledding? Are you good at that?" Daniel added.

Anna admitted that she enjoyed sledding very much, but that she had never played baseball.

"Margaret is very good at it," Daniel bragged.

Russell shot his wife a surprised look. She grinned with self-satisfaction. "The boys say I'm one of the best," she boasted playfully.

Russell grinned. "Oh really?"

"Yes. Your mother is quite a ball player too," Margaret continued.

Joanna beamed as George nodded agreement.

"Goodness! You would never know it by the looks of you," Missus Simpson spoke gently. "You're all fine and lady-like. Did you really play a man's sporting game?"

Margaret nodded. "Yes ma'am, we did, but not in our fancy clothes. We put on work dresses and had some fine fun getting a little dirty."

Anna's mother sighed in relief. She was glad that Joanna Chadwick was a down-to-earth woman. She had worried that the Chadwicks might be high and mighty with all their money and a comfortable life.

When the food arrived, everyone ate fairly quickly. It was decided that the Simpsons as well as Russell, Margaret and the boys, should return home before dark. The air was turning colder and the sky grew dark with snow clouds. Sure enough, sometime during the night, a light snow began to fall. When the time came for the dinner party on Christmas Eve, at least six inches covered the ground. No one arrived on time. Margaret began to worry.

"Do you think something is wrong, Russell?" she asked her husband.

"No. They are only fifteen minutes late. Let's give them a little more time before we go looking for everyone," he suggested. "Ma could have changed her dress at the last minute or they might have been held up at Anna's house. You just never know."

Margaret spent an anxious five minutes looking out the window. Finally, a closed carriage came up the road. Henry sat in the driver's seat swiftly guiding the animals along the drive. "They're here," Margaret announced with relief.

Russell pulled on a coat to greet his guests. Henry was jumping down when Russell stepped out and opened the carriage. Only Anna sat inside. A small coal stove warmed the interior of the carriage, but Anna did have a blanket on the bench just in case.

"Welcome," Russell greeted as he reached to help her down.

"Thank you," Anna told him.

"Where is everyone else?" Russell then asked.

Henry replied, "They decided to stay in town. Pa didn't want to get out in this weather and mother didn't have the heart to leave him alone. They send their regards."

"You two go on in and get warm," Russell offered. "I'll see to the horses."

Anna and Henry hurried up the front porch steps. Margaret waited at the door to greet them. "Come in." She gave them both a hug. They were both surprisingly warm. "It was such a good idea to get a closed carriage," Margaret complimented Henry. "Anna, you are warm as a toasted bun. Henry, does warm air come to the driver too? You hardly seem cold at all."

"Uh…no," Henry stammered. Margaret glanced at Anna, who was now a nice shade of crimson. It was then that Margaret noticed Anna's coat, and how the buttons were not closed correctly. One of her eyebrows shot up curiously.

"I just drove really fast from the Simpson house," Henry fibbed.

Margaret thought that was a terrible lie, but said nothing. She only shook her head slightly. They must have stopped along the road to kiss in private. Thank goodness they were getting married tomorrow.

"Well, come in and make yourselves comfortable. I will pull dinner out of the oven."

Margaret could hear her guests removing their coats. She only smiled slightly when Anna let out a small gasp. No doubt she had discovered the missed button hole.

"Is it time to eat yet?" Daniel's voice called down the stairwell.

Margaret hollered back. "Yep. Wash up."

Russell returned from the barn and the family all sat around the table to say grace. Soon after, all conversation centered around tomorrow's big event.

Christmas morning arrived quietly with its magical charm. Margaret woke in a warm bed with a crackling fire. Russell seemed to be fast asleep by her side. He looked very festive in his bright red union suit. Margaret assumed he had risen earlier to add more wood to the fire. The room was toasty warm as she slipped from bed to quietly dress. She would get downstairs early to prepare a good breakfast. Maybe later this morning she and Russell would give the boys their gifts. Somehow, she had managed to sew them each a new shirt between Thanksgiving and Christmas. She hoped they liked them. Both were made from thick blue cotton.

Trying not to make a sound, Margaret turned the door knob. Wearing only woolen socks, she was able to walk down the stairs without making a sound. That was, until she got to the bottom.

"Russell!" she shrieked with excitement. She scampered back up the stairs and threw open the bedroom door. Russell sat in bed, grinning at her like the cat who ate the canary.

"How do you like it?" he questioned, knowing full well the answer already.

"A tree, Russell? When? How? I've never had a Christmas tree of my own to decorate," she admitted with more excitement than pity.

"Well, you have one now. I cut it down two days ago and snuck it in this morning. I thought we could all decorate it after breakfast," he suggested.

Daniel and Johnny curiously popped their heads out the door to their room. "What's going on?" Daniel asked sleepily.

"Yeah. Why did you scream?" Johnny asked Margaret.

"Because your brother got us a tree," she replied enthusiastically. "Isn't that great? We can decorate it after breakfast." Margaret leaned over and gave Russell a big kiss on the mouth. "Thank you dear, and Merry Christmas."

Russell smiled. "Merry Christmas to you too. And…you're welcome. See you downstairs," he winked.

Smiling, Margaret skipped back downstairs to begin her work in the kitchen. Every now and then, she would stop and walk into the parlor, just to look at her first real tree. It would need bows and presents. Once she got the coffee going, she would dig the three gifts out of hiding. Only then would she start the bacon, eggs and biscuits.

When Russell came down the stairwell, his footsteps sounded different. Margaret wondered what was going on. She could hear the boys snickering too. "What are you fellows up to?" she questioned with her hands covered in flour.

Russell emerged from behind the wall, with an enormous box in his arms. A large ribbon bow sat neatly on top. "Merry Christmas dear," he repeated.

Margaret stopped short. "My, oh my! What is it?"

"Open it Margaret," Johnny urged.

She wiped her hands on a dish towel and hurried to the gift which now rested on the floor near the tree. Russell noticed the other gifts wrapped in brown paper.

"Looks like I'm not the only one with a gift," he spoke

The boys eagerly looked around him to locate names on the gift tags.

"This one's mine!" Johnny shouted, picking up the soft bundle.

Daniel picked his up and shook it. Russell eyed his suspiciously.

"Well, should we all stand here wondering, or should we open them?" Margaret asked. Immediately there was a mad scramble for gifts. Paper tore as the boys discovered their newly sewn shirts. Russell was just as bad. Within ten seconds his new coat was out of its wrapping too.

"Did you make this?" he asked Margaret. "When did you have time?"

Margaret nodded proudly. "I made it in the fall, when you were outside working."

"It's a fine coat, dear. And the fit is perfect," he complimented. Truly, he was impressed with her fine handiwork. The coat was warm and heavy, lined with goosedown. It would surely keep him warm on even the coldest days. "Now what of your gift?" he asked.

"I can't get the top off."

Russell and the boys helped pull up the lid to the large crate. When it popped off, Margaret began to dig through the packing material. Her fingers touched something metal. She tried to pull, but it was too heavy.

"Help me get this stuff out," she requested of them all. They each grabbed handfuls of the straw. Margaret's eyes were surprised when she saw the treasure underneath. It was a sewing machine. "Oh Russell, I love it!" she shouted.

Russell and his brothers pulled out the equipment. Margaret watched as they set up the table with the machine built in. It was top of the line, the best one in the catalog. She could hardly believe it. It would cut her sewing time by more than half. How fun it would be to make her next dress.

"Thank you so much!" she gushed as she hugged him.

"I thought you would like it. I know how long it takes you to make things by hand."

Margaret was genuinely touched by his thoughtfulness. He was growing more dear to her with every week. Even if he still could not tell her that he loved her, she was starting to love him.

"Well, shall we feed the animals boys, so Margaret can feed us?" Russell suggested. The boys ran upstairs to put on their coats, hats and gloves.

After the good hot meal, Margaret, Russell and the boys decorated the tree. Russell popped corn, which the boys then strung on sewing thread. Margaret cut strips of scrap material and tied bows on the branches. She thought the finished product was a cheerful looking country Christmas tree.

"Looks rather puny, don't you think?" Russell asked everyone.

She shook her head. "No. Not to me."

"Still, I think next year, we should buy some glass ornaments at the store," he stated, scratching his chin. "Oh, boys, I almost forgot. There is another present for you out in the barn."

Daniel and Johnny turned on their heels and raced to put on coats and gloves again. Brother raced brother outside to be the first one into the barn. Margaret gave Russell a curious look.

"It's a sled," he whispered once the boys were out of earshot. "It should keep them busy until after noon. What time do we have to be there?"

Margaret sighed. She had already told him at least three times. Apparently he had not been listening. "I am needed at the church no later than three. However, I think your parents wanted us to join them at the hotel beforehand so we could exchange gifts. We best leave here at one, to be safe."

Russell nodded, then ran out to see if the boys liked their gift. He was going to show them exactly how to use it. Margaret watched as the trio of males walked away to find the perfect hill. Deep in her heart, Margaret knew that Russell would be good with children. Maybe one day they would have some.

By one o'clock, Margaret stood waiting in the parlor wearing her reddish-orange velvet dress. Over this she wore her warm coat. The fur muff and hat rested on a nearby table. As expected, the boys, including Russell, were late in returning from their sledding adventure. Each was rosy cheeked, but grinning widely as they entered the house. Margaret impatiently tapped her foot and urged them to hurry. "We're late!" she warned.

To pass time, she glanced over the gifts on the table. Some were for Christmas, others were wedding presents. For Joanna, George and Henry, she had newly embroidered handkerchiefs. For a wedding gift, she had pre-paid a photographer in town to take a portrait of the bride and groom. Her receipt was in a pretty envelope tied with velvet ribbon. Also wrapped was a store bought sampler which said 'Home Sweet Home' for the newlyweds to hang in their house.

Three sets of feet finally stomped down the stairs, alerting Margaret that they were ready. "I was beginning to worry we might not make it," she teased.

"You should have been there! We were on this great big hill and rushed down to the bottom in just seconds," Daniel explained all in one breath.

"Maybe I can go with you next time," she said. Johnny's face seemed sullen. "What's the matter, Johnny?"

"I just remembered. Russell said we had to leave the sled here when we go home," he pouted.

Margaret turned to her husband. "Is that true?"

He nodded. "I thought it would be a good way to get them to come back next year. Besides, you and I might enjoy it."

Margaret rolled her eyes as everyone filed out the door and into the yard. At least Russell had already hitched up the team. They all piled into the wagon and covered with blankets. Margaret placed the gifts beneath the seat and thanked the good Lord above that it had stopped snowing.

The drive into town was enjoyable. The foursome spoke with such gaiety, the trip hardly seemed as long as usual. Before they knew it, Russell pulled in front of the hotel. Once he helped Margaret onto solid ground, he told her, "You go inside. I'm going to take the horses to the livery. Be back in a few."

When Russell returned, he found his entire family waiting for him in an upstairs parlor. Tempting presents were laid out on a table, just waiting to be opened. Russell took his rightful seat beside Margaret. George said a few words about the blessings of Christmas and thanked God for the family and all their blessings. He then asked God to bring him some grandchildren. At this, Margaret gulped. She wondered if Russell would say anything about it later. After the "Amen" the melee began. Adults and children alike dove for their gifts. Margaret was pleased to find a small pair of pearl earrings shaped like flowers, embossed stationery, and a book of poems. Russell received a new gold watch chain, a fine pair of leather gloves, and a new farmer's almanac. Hugs and kisses were given freely as everyone thanked everyone for their gifts. Daniel and Johnny immediately set up the game board received from their parents. With it, one could play either checkers or chess. Russell and Henry were too eager to help them with their strategy. Margaret and Joanna sat themselves in a corner to discuss the wedding. George went over to watch the game.

By three o'clock, when the women left to help decorate the church, it was obvious that Henry was starting to get nervous. He glanced at his watch every ten minutes or less.

"Calm down, son. It will get here soon enough," George tried to soothe him."

Henry loosened his collar. Three hours to go and he would be a married man. He hoped he lived up to Anna's expectations. Until the summer, they would live with his parents. But after that, they would be moving into a home ten miles east, closer to Chicago. George had convinced Henry to open another store closer to the heart of the city. "You can manage it fine by yourself," his father had said. Henry was pleased that his father had so much confidence in him. He wished he had it in himself at this particular moment.

The time came for everyone to get to the church. Gathering supplies, they headed out into the cold.

Meanwhile, Anna, her mother, Margaret, Joanna and Susan Grady decorated the church. Green and red paper streamers draped the walls. Dried flower arrangements hung from the top of each inverted crescent. A clean red carpet lay along the center aisle. On the inner side of each pew hung an elaborate bow made from red streamer paper. It was simply done, but elegant for a Christmas wedding. After the ceremony, Susan Grady had offered her adjacent home for a reception. Her dining table was covered in delightful treats prepared by Anna, her friends, and her mother's friends. Susan helped too.

At present, Anna was inside Susan's home putting on the elaborate wedding gown. The women were in attendance to help. Margaret noticed how very quiet the home was without Susan's little boy. "Where is he, by the way?" she asked.

"Missus Meade is watching him for the day," Susann answered. "She is such a gift. And in a few more months, she will be invaluable," she added.

Margaret wrinkled up her brow. "What do you mean, Susan? Is there something you need to tell us?"

Susan smiled as if she were the keeper of a great secret. "Well, Reverend Grady and I are expecting a new addition to the family."

All the women cooed over this exciting news. "Congratulations. So happy for you. How wonderful," they all echoed.

"When is the baby due?" Anna asked innocently.

Susan replied, "In about six months."

Conversation over the new baby was dropped within minutes as Pastor Grady came for the women. "It's time ladies," he announced after tapping the door.

The room grew quiet. Anna gulped. This was the moment she had been waiting for. She was so excited and so nervous all at the same time. Tonight she would become Missus Henry Chadwick. How wonderful!!!!

10

A simple piano played out the sounds of the wedding march. Anna stepped regally down the red carpet. Henry's breath caught short in his throat. She was incredible. So sweet and majestic, and beautiful. All nervousness disappeared as his wonderful bride took her place by his side.

Anna smiled up at her beloved Henry. He would be good to her. She could see it on his face. He was so very handsome in his black suit too. She could hardly wait for the kiss. At the thought, she blushed, and tried to focus on Reverend Grady.

Pastor Grady read from the Bible. He then read the vows, which Henry and Anna repeated in turn. No one messed up. Henry placed a ring on his bride's finger and the Pastor announced them man and wife. "You may kiss your bride."

Anna gulped again and smiled nervously as Henry lifted the single layer of netting which covered her face. Her eyes shone brightly and her smile warm enough to melt ice. Henry cupped her chin gently and bent down to offer his new wife a tender, loving kiss.

At least forty-five friends and neighbors clapped and cheered for the newlyweds. The piano began to play again as the pair faced the congregation. After all the congratulations, the photographer took their picture at the altar. Friends stayed to watch before walking over to the Grady's home for food and fellowship.

The reception was grand, and lasted over three hours. The six o'clock wedding had taken only twenty minutes. Anna's childhood friends wished her well. Some wept with happiness, others with jealousy. After much eating and socializing, Henry and Anna began to open gifts that were piled high on a nearby table. It was such fun discovering what treasure lay inside. There were kitchen items, towels and fancy spoons and such, lace doilies, figurines and frames. Some gave mirrors, baskets and bowls.

By the end of the evening, everyone was exhausted. Henry and Anna were anxious to get away and be alone. Without much ceremony, they bid everyone a goodnight and slipped out of sight. Once the guests of honor left, the party broke apart. Many bundled up and left before the cleaning began. Margaret stayed an extra half hour, putting dishes into the kitchen and sorting out what was left of the food. Mister Simpson was crying when he and his wife left. He felt like he had lost his little girl. Margaret watched the tender scene with sadness in her heart. Anna was lucky to have a father who loved her so much.

When it was time, Russell and the boys went for the wagon and horses at the livery. "Do come out to the house tomorrow," she invited her in-laws.

"As long as the snow isn't blowing, we'll be there," George promised. He waved goodbye with his hat in the air and ventured out into the cold wintry night. At least his walk to the hotel was a short one.

Cold bits of icy air swirled about the wagon in a bitter wind as Russell drove toward home. He would have to go quickly because he feared the clouds would burst forth at any moment. It would not do to be caught in a blizzard tonight. With a lantern on each side of the wagon, he hurried down the road. The horses were all too happy to oblige. They didn't want to be out in this cold night air either. Just ahead was their home barn with hay and warmth.

All of Iowa City woke the next morning to a thick blanket of new white snow. Even more fell silently as fires were rekindled for breakfast. After sleeping in later than usual, Johnny and Daniel bounded down the stairs ready to test the fresh snow with their sled.

"Not so fast, boys!" Margaret warned lovingly. "You have to eat a warm breakfast first. So sit down."

The boys did as they were told, but did nothing to hide their impatience. Russell tried to hide his grin behind a steaming cup of coffee. In order to lessen their sorrow of having been scolded, he made a suggestion. "I have an idea. When you two get back from sledding, I challenge you to a game of checkers. You two against me. Are we on?"

"But that's not fair to you Russ," Daniel reasoned.

Russell shrugged. "It's a risk I am willing to take." He gave Margaret a playful wink.

Margaret approached the table carrying a tray of food. A thought jumped into her mind and came out before she could catch it. "I don't know what made me think of this Russell, but Susan and her husband are expecting another baby."

"Really? Jack didn't mention it yesterday," he replied.

Margaret chuckled. "I didn't think babies were something men discussed on a regular basis."

Russell actually blushed just one shade of pink as he looked away. Truly, he was embarrassed at having broached such a female subject. He cleared his throat after glancing at his brothers. Both boys were staring at him, wide-eyed.

Not much else was spoken until all the plates were served and Russell had spoken a prayer. Russell took an enormous bite so his mouth could say no more.

"I heard Ma and Pa talking about a woman who was with child," Daniel sated in a grown up manner. "They said she died trying to have the baby. They didn't know I could hear them from the other room."

Margaret and Russell looked at Daniel in surprise. "Daniel, that wasn't nice to eavesdrop," Russell scolded in a calm voice.

Daniel defended himself. "I wasn't doing it on purpose. I was reading a book in my room and I heard them talking in the hallway. I couldn't help but hear every word."

"How sad for that poor young woman and her husband," Margaret spoke quietly. "I wonder if…" she didn't dare speak her thoughts about the baby's life Surely, if the mother died, the baby must have too. Margaret offered a quick prayer for Susan and her unborn child.

"Poor nothing! She was rich. Very, very rich. And conceited too," Daniel continued.

Margaret was shocked. "Daniel? How can you say such a terrible thing? Did you even know her?"

"Yes, ma'am. I did. It was Ethel," he answered without pause.

Margaret's heart jumped into her throat. She looked at Russell in alarm.

Russell could hardly believe his ears. His body went numb. His entire being seemed to drop into the pit of his stomach, or maybe the floor. He felt sick. He gulped back the nausea and turned to Daniel. Trying not to vomit, he asked in a soft voice, "Are you sure it was Ethel?"

"Quite sure. I heard Ma say her name more than once," he replied.

Russell stood up quickly, knocking his chair down in the process. A sob of anguish escaped his mouth as he ran upstairs. When Margaret heard the door slam shut, the tears fell from her own eyes. She knew Russell was crying too, but not for the same reason. He still loved Ethel, or the memory of her at least. Margaret offered the boys an apologetic smile and dabbed at her tears with a napkin.

"What did I say?" Daniel asked innocently. He was very upset about his brother's reaction.

"Ethel was his first love Daniel. Part of him still cares for her," was all she dared to say. If she told him that Ethel was Russell's only love, that might get back to their parents. It would only make matters worse.

"But...I thought he hated her for walking out on him. That's why he moved way out here. I thought he wouldn't care. Honest..." Daniel said with his bottom lip quivering. His heart felt terrible. He might even cry too.

Margaret just wasn't sure how to feel. A very tiny part of her actually agreed with Daniel at being happy about Ethel's death. Margaret knew it was wrong to feel that way, but Ethel was the root of her continuing problems with Russell. However, this month had been a good one. Maybe now that Ethel was truly gone, Russell could forget about her and move on. Surely he could find room in his heart for his real wife as well.

"Boys, you finish eating and go on outside for a while. I will talk to your brother, Daniel, and let him know you didn't mean anything by it." Margaret left her mostly full plate on the table. Her appetite was gone completely. She busied herself with the dishes while the boys finished eating. Once they were outside, she decided to go upstairs.

Margaret opened the door to the room. Russell sat at his desk, his head rested in folded arms. When he heard her enter, he looked up, wiping red puffy eyes. "She's gone, Margaret. I can't believe she's really gone. She was so pretty. It's just not fair," he moaned pitifully.

Margaret felt greatly unloved at this moment. Here was her husband, pining away for a lost love, when she herself in the flesh stood before him. He was cruel. What good was her affection for him when it was not returned? What good was a marriage without reciprocated love? It was no marriage at all. Standing stiffly in their room, Margaret made the decision to give Russell a few days to grieve. Then, she would offer him a choice: marriage, or freedom.

Luckily, the snow kept Russell's parents from visiting that day. Margaret entertained the boys while Russell kept to himself upstairs. The night was no better. Russell tossed and turned in the bed, making a poor night for sleep. And each time he called out Ethel's name, Margaret felt an invisible dagger pierce her heart. By morning, her mood was anything but pleasant.

When George and Joanna arrived at noon, the boys were greatly relieved to have a happy distraction. "Pa, will you play a game with us?" Johnny begged while holding up the chess board.

"What sour faces you boys have. I thought for sure you would have fun out here in the country," he answered. George sat down and obliged them one game.

"Margaret, you look positively exhausted. Have the boys worn you out that much?" Joanna asked worriedly. The young woman looked fatigued so much that she swayed when she stood. "Here, let me help you with that." Joanna grabbed the big pot of stew and set it on the hook over the fire. "Where is Russell?"

Margaret managed a weak smile. "He is upstairs. I will get him," she replied flatly.

"Is he ill? Are you ill?" Joanna was getting really worried now. "Is everything all right, Margaret?"

"We're just tired, that's all. It's been a busy week."

Margaret slowly climbed the stairwell and tapped on the door before turning the knob. Russell lay across the bed still wearing his union suit. He looked miserable. Margaret spoke softly. "Russ, your parents are here. I have a stew on for dinner if you want to join us." That is all she said before leaving quietly. Margaret forced a smile for her mother-in-law. "He should be down soon. Let me get the bread in and I will join you in the parlor."

Ten minutes later, Russell made his appearance. He wore overalls and a simple shirt. It was obvious by his red eyes that he had been crying. Joanna stood in alarm. "Russell Chadwick, you tell me right now what's wrong?"

Russell glanced quickly at everyone in the room, including his wife. Then he slumped down into a comfortable chair. His eyes stared catatonically into the fire. "I found out about Ethel," he finally spoke.

"Oh!" Joanna exclaimed, taking a quick worried look at Margaret. Did Russell's new wife know about Ethel? Apparently so, Margaret looked positively green. Joanna's heart fell. How had Russell found out? Who had told him about his former fiancé's death?

"We felt it best not to tell you," George stated. "You have a lovely new wife now, and a good life. Things are back on track, and you're happy. No use dredging up the past, I say…"

Russell stared off into the flames again.

Joanna looked to Margaret. Her daughter-in-law was speechless. Joanna too, for once, was at a loss for words.

Russell moved in his chair. "Did the baby live?"

Joanna looked to George. Should she tell her son the truth?

George saw Joanna's alarm, and Margaret's heartbreak. "Russ, let's you and me take a walk outside for a minute," he suggested. He stood and walked toward his son. He was not going to take no for an answer.

When Russell joined his father on the snowy front lawn, he learned the terrible truth about Ethel's last day. She had been in painful labor for twenty hours. Finally, she had delivered a stillborn son. Shortly thereafter, she had succumbed to the rigors of childbirth, and joined her baby in heaven.

Once again, Russell's eyes filled with tears. There was so much sorrow in his heart, he could hardly cope. "If she had married me Pa, she might still be alive today. She was supposed to have my children. I just don't know what I did wrong. Why did I lose her? Why didn't she love me enough?" He choked out a few sobs. "This is so wrong. It's just not fair!" he wailed like a spoiled child.

George listened to his son's words with confusion. It was obvious now, that he still loved Ethel. What on earth had made him marry Margaret? That poor sweet girl. His son was treating her so meanly. After another breath, George grew angry. "Not fair to whom, son? To Ethel? To you? Or to Margaret?" he boomed. "How do you think she is feeling right now with you acting this way? I don't feel sorry for you, and you had better stop feeling sorry for yourself or you are going to lose the best thing that's ever happened to you. Margaret is fantastic. And you're a fool if you can't see that!"

Russell watched out of the corner of his eye as his father stormed off. What did he know? He had never lost his love. He had never known heartache like this. Joanna had been his first and only love. He had committed his heart to her at eighteen and never wavered. This ran deep, deeper than anyone knew.

After some time, Russell returned to the warm house. He was freezing from being outside for so long and his body was simply drained of energy. Bowls of stew sat in order on the table and Margaret was just setting down the bread. His younger brothers eyed him curiously, but Russell avoided eye contact with the adults. He stared at the bowl without appetite.

George offered a prayer. It was simple. "Lord bless this food to our bodies, lift our spirits. We thank Thee for all Thy blessings. Amen."

The boys dug in, but the grown-ups were weary. No one said a word, until Joanna finally spoke. "Boys, I think it would be fun if you came to the hotel with us tonight. Don't you think, dear?"

"Oh yes, indeed," George bellowed with a nod. Maybe if his son and daughter-in-law had the house to themselves, they could talk about this problem. Hopefully, his son would come to his senses. Margaret was worth ten of Ethel. She was worthy of Russell's love, if only he was willing.

Margaret was grateful for her in-laws presence. The meal would have been unbearable without them and the afternoon in the parlor would have been miserable. As it was, Joanna kept it light and friendly, and helped prevent Margaret's mood from sinking into some dark place.

"I wonder what Anna and Henry are up to right now," she said without thinking.

"I'm sure we don't want to know," George scolded.

Johnny suddenly jumped up. "Why don't we all go out for some rides on the sled?"

Given the heavy weight of Ethel's death which hung in the air, everyone but Russell accepted Johnny's invitation.

"I think I'll just stay here and keep the fires going," he told them dully. It was probably best. He was not good company.

Margaret pulled on her warmest coat, hat, scarf, gloves and boots. It would be good to go sledding today. She needed to smile for even half an hour. Besides, if she left Russell and ended the marriage, this might be her last chance to play with his family. They had been wonderful to her from day one.

Two hours were spent outside enjoying the snow. George only went down the hill a few times, letting his boys make the most of their gift. After a few tries, he returned to the house because the cold hurt his bones. Joanna and Margaret enjoyed themselves tremendously, forgetting all their problems in the few seconds it took to slide down the ice. Johnny and Daniel fell over laughing when their mother and sister-in-law went down together and flipped the sled, finishing the hill on their backs with their legs and petticoats up in the air. Margaret laughed so hard she cried. It was a great way to get out tears without anyone knowing her heart was breaking.

Around four in the afternoon, the cold foursome headed back. Margaret promised them all hot tea and biscuits with jelly. Joanna declined her invitation to stay for supper. "It's getting dark much too fast. George will want to return to the hotel soon for a hot bath."

A hot bath. That sounded good to Margaret too. If she was able to speak to Russell later, she would ask him to bring in the tub. Maybe a good soak would ease some troubles away as well.

As expected, George took his family to town. Margaret asked Russell for the tub in as few words as possible. He brought it in without conversation.

"I don't feel like fixing supper tonight," Margaret explained.

"I ain't hungry either," Russell replied. "I'll be upstairs in the room."

"Just so you know, I will be sleeping in the guest room tonight. So let me get my things before you fall asleep," Margaret spoke, trying to keep the bitter edge out of her words. Deep down, she had hoped he would ask for her forgiveness. Say he was sorry, ask her to stay in their shared room, anything.

Russell nodded and allowed his wife to go upstairs first. Margaret grabbed her bathing supplies and clothing. Without another word, she left the room. Russell entered and closed the door behind him.

Feeling low and dejected, Margaret piled her things on the kitchen table. She filled a large kettle with water and placed it on the swing arm over the fire. She then lit the stove and placed three more large pots of water on top to warm. For the last two days, she had held back her emotions. Now that she was alone in the kitchen, she allowed herself to cry. All the hurt and disappointment in her heart came out in the form of large salty tears which slid down her cheeks. She hugged herself and rocked back and forth at the kitchen table. The sobs came freely and without end. Russell had put on a good show these last few weeks. He had really deceived her, deceived everyone. He had made her think that he cared. What a lie. Margaret had never felt more alone in all her life. She mourned her lost chance to find love and happiness. There was no love in his heart, at least none for her. Margaret sobbed over her lot in life. It had not presented her with much happiness. She had taken what she could in these last few months, enjoying the time with his parents. She and Russell had even found a few occasions to be lighthearted, but they had been few and far between. And now, she realized, all the affection they had shared, had been a ruse.

Taking a deep, slow breath, Margaret began to undress. She would get clean. She would cleanse herself from all this unhappiness and make a plan for her future. She had some big decisions to make. If she had to give up on love, so be it. She could harden her heart and stop expecting affection. It would be up to her now to find and make some happiness in this world. She would not enjoy leaving this home though; she had made it her own. She had made it comfortable. Everywhere she looked, her touch was apparent, from the homemade curtains, to the candle-wicked pillows resting on the stuffed chairs. From the rugs, to the lamps, to the items on the walls, it was all her doing.

Margaret let down her long red hair. It felt soft against the small of her back. Taking a little glass bottle, she emptied the contents into the bath water. The kitchen took on the smell of lavender. Next, Margaret emptied the warm water vessels into the tub. She then stepped into the steaming pool, which was almost too hot. Once her body adjusted to the temperature, she leaned back and closed her eyes. Wiping a few more tears, she tried to relax and block out all her troubled thoughts. Breathe. All she had to do right now was breathe.

The bath helped. Margaret soaked until the water turned tepid. Then quickly, she washed all over. Her hair was dried slowly as she sat in front of the fire in her room. She wore a warm flannel gown and simply breathed to pass the time. There was no noise at all from Russell's room. She figured he was asleep, unable to face her, or the truth. A small part of her heart and mind wondered if he considered her feelings at all in this matter.

Mentally and physically exhausted, Margaret crawled into bed. In the morning, she would have that talk with Russell and give him his options.

11

The house was eerily silent when Margaret's eyes opened the next morning. Her head ached with pain. She would take some medicine with breakfast. That would help.

She dressed slowly. The thought of having her hair up in a tight twist only increased her pain, so she opted to plait the length of it and let it fall loose down her back. When Margaret opened the bedroom door, she noticed that Russell's door was open too. He was not in his room through. At the bottom of the steps, Margaret was shocked to see that the clock hands showed nine-thirty. She had never slept that late in her life.

Breakfast was toast and milk. Russell had at least milked the cows before going wherever he went. She wondered where he was. By nightfall, Margaret was still wondering. A horse was missing from the barn, so he had gone somewhere. Maybe to talk with a friend. But shouldn't he be back by now? It was dark. There was no word from Mister and Missus Chadwick either. Margaret grew both annoyed and worried.

When morning arrived and there was still no sign of her husband, Margaret was greatly distressed. Had he done something drastic? She feared for his life, given his state of sorrow. Dressing quickly in warm clothing, she hurried to the barn to saddle the other horse. She could ride him into town much faster than taking the wagon. Kicking a boot into the stirrup, Margaret pulled herself into the saddle. She needed to check with her in-laws. Maybe they knew something. Tapping her heels into the horse's sides, she galloped toward town.

Margaret found all the Chadwicks in the hotel parlor. Even Anna and Henry sat together, smiling.

"Have you seen Russell?" she asked without any formalities.

Everyone shook their head. "What's wrong, dear?" Joanna asked.

George stood. "What happened?"

Margaret shared what she knew. Russell had left early yesterday morning and had not returned. She feared for his life. A search party was immediately organized. Johnny and Daniel were to notify Minister Grady, then make inquiries around town. George and Henry decided to search the surrounding area, including the river.

"You don't think..." Joanna asked in a hushed voice as her hand came to her throat.

"I don't know what to think. We just have to search everywhere," her husband replied.

Margaret, Anna and Joanna were to wait at the hotel. It was much too cold for them to be outside for long, the men had said. In truth, they each realized that the men were trying to protect them from a possibly unpleasant experience.

"My poor boy!" Joanna cried into her handkerchief.

"Why would he do such a thing?" Anna asked, ignorant of the events which had transpired over the past few days.

With a sad deep breath, Margaret filled her in while Joanna continued to weep. She tried to tell her friend only what she needed to know, but apparently, she explained more than Joanna knew.

Her eyes popped open with disbelief. "He did that to you?"

With a twist in her heart, Margaret nodded.

Joanna frowned. "If they find that boy alive, I'll give him a thing or two to think about. What a fool I raised!" she nearly yelled.

The sadness over Russell's disappearance was lifted temporarily, in their anger. But the hours ticked by slowly as the three women waited for news. Finally at five in the evening, George and Henry returned. No one had seen Russell. There was not a trace of news about him. After warming briefly, they set out again in search of the boys.

"We have news!" George's strong voice called as he walked through the doors at seven.

"I found out where he went," Daniel said proudly of his sleuthing efforts.

All female eyes focused on the men.

"He got on a train heading East," George explained. "I can only assume he is headed home."

A sigh of relief emitted from both Margaret and Joanna. At least he was alive.

"When did he board?" Margaret questioned.

"Yesterday. We've wired to Chicago and Wheaton to see if he has been seen, or whether or not he has purchased a return ticket. They will send an answer to the hotel in the morning," Henry explained.

"Now we just wait?" Joanna asked with annoyance.

"This is all we can do. Margaret, you are welcome to stay with us tonight if you like. It will save you the trip home and back," George suggested.

"Thank you. I think I will." The animals wouldn't be happy, but they would survive one night.

A private supper was ordered for the entire family. They ate in their suite of rooms. It had been a long weary day. Margaret was again besieged by an awful headache. The strain of events was more than she could bear. Joanna put Margaret to bed in her room. George and the boys would share in the other. Henry and his bride returned to their hotel down the street.

When word came the following morning that Russell had not purchased a return ticket, it was decided by all to return to Wheaton.

"The week is nearly over anyway," George said factually. "We might as well go back and search for him."

Joanna, George and the boys left that very day for home. Margaret, Anna and Henry would leave tomorrow. Anna wanted one more day to say goodbye to her parents before leaving for her new home. Margaret had to pack her bags and make arrangements for the animals to be cared for.

When she entered the home, it was so very quiet. She surveyed the rooms carefully before closing her eyes. She was standing at the threshold of a very important decision. Taking a deep breath, Margaret decided to go through with it. Why not? She only had a house to lose. Margaret pulled her trunk out of storage and began to fill it with every item she owned. Not only did she fill it, but also her small traveling bag which had accompanied her across three states this past summer.

Two days ago, she had planned to give Russell a choice in deciding her future. But today, she had decided that he had not earned a vote. He had no say in the matter anymore. Taking flight and leaving her alone was answer enough. He wanted nothing to do with her. She would go to town early tomorrow and file for a divorce. Once she reached Chicago, she would find work.

Having made up her mind, Margaret thought she would sleep well. However, she tossed and turned all night. It was a great relief when morning came. She would get her plans underway before she lost her nerve. She did not want to turn back to a loveless marriage. She wanted to look forward to her future.

Margaret managed to load the heavy trunk onto the wagon with a great deal of effort, two planks, a horse and some rope. She rode into town and dropped off the trunk at the station, then led the horse to an attorney's office, where she filed for divorce. The man inside informed her that the paperwork would require her husband's signature.

"I have no doubt he will sign it, as soon as I can find him," she told the attorney.

Margaret stabled the horse and wagon at the livery. Grabbing her one small bag, she then headed to the station to wait for Henry and Anna. It would be so hard to say goodbye to the family. They were wonderful, and had grown very dear to her. She was sure they cared for her as well, but it was not the family to whom she was married. It was their no good son. And Margaret would not be saddled with a cruel man for the rest of her life. She fought back tears as she stepped into the building.

It was warm inside. She took a seat and glanced at the clock. One hour until the train. Margaret took a deep steadying breath. This first step was the hardest. Once she boarded the train, the rest would be easy. At least, she hoped so.

The journey to Wheaton was uneventful. When the train arrived at the station, an anxious faced Henry scanned the crowd for his father. "There he is. In the tall hat."

George was pushing through the crowd with an eager look on his face. "I have news," he spoke in a rush. "He has been found!" He took a breath, then added, "By the police this morning. He is alive, but very ill. They have him at the hospital. We can go there right away."

"Let me arrange for our trunks Father," Henry spoke. "I will meet you there."

George and the women quickly walked away. When Henry met with the family half an hour later, their faces were grim.

"He has a very high fever. They say he must have been outside for at least the last forty-eight hours. The next twenty-four are very critical," Joanna spoke with seriousness.

"Where did they find him," Henry questioned.

"In the graveyard, son. He was lying on top of Ethel's grave," George answered with a knot in his stomach. It made him sick to say this in front of Margaret, but what else could he do?

Henry felt a tiny bit sorry for his brother at this point. He must truly have been tormented by her death to go through such extreme measures to be near her. Henry wondered how Margaret would handle all this. Surely it was a blow. She sat unmoving on a bench, staring at the floor.

Margaret knew she had to keep herself together. She could not let these people see how very deeply her heart was aching. She sat as still as possible, not wanting to do anything except breathe. Part of her still cared for Russell, a very little part, so she would stay until his life was out of danger. But since she knew that their future together was impossible, she would make an exit as quietly as possible.

It was determined an hour later that some of the family should go home. Margaret volunteered for the first shift concluding privately that Russell was least likely to come to during the next few hours. Everyone assumed she did it out of wifely duty, and so agreed.

Margaret ordered a pot of black coffee to be sent up to the room and sat down in the hard chair in the corner. She was to send word to the family if there were any changes in this condition. The night wore on. Margaret dozed in the chair off and on. At one point, Russell began to moan and call out.

"Don't leave me, my love. Please don't leave me," he begged.

"I'm here, Russell," Margaret answered sleepily.

"Oh, Ethel. I thought you had gone," he replied before returning to a restful sleep.

Margaret notified the nurse that Russell had come to for a short time. "He was talking to me, but called me by the wrong name."

The nurse nodded. "That happens sometimes. Patients sometimes hallucinate when suffering a high fever. He is out of his mind right now. But don't worry, ma'am, once he recovers, he will be himself again."

That was no consolation. Margaret kept her thoughts to herself. He would know her in the morning, but he wouldn't want her. She was the wrong woman. It would be better, she decided, if she gave him his freedom. Margaret turned to the nurse. "Do you have any paper and a pen I can use?"

"Yes, ma'am. Come to my station."

When George arrived early the next morning, Margaret had completed her letter. It was for Russell when he was coherent. It explained the divorce papers filed back in Iowa and why she was leaving. She said it was unfair to them both to continue the marriage. Margaret wished him well and told him that she hoped he would be happy again one day.

"Any change?" George asked.

"He woke up once last night, but he didn't see me," she answered.

"That has to be a good sign, eh?" George smiled. "Daniel is downstairs waiting to take you home. Looks like you could use some sleep."

Margaret thanked him kindly and made her way down the steps. Maybe, in a day or two, she would be able to give Russell the letter and make her departure.

The sad wife remained at her in-laws' home until the next morning. Henry sent word that Russell was showing signs of life, so everyone rode eagerly to the hospital. Everyone except for Margaret, that is. So this was it, the day she said goodbye. Her head throbbed and she felt sick. Margaret hoped she had the nerve to go through with her plan. She squeezed her hands into fists, nervously.

Russell was sipping broth when they entered his room. He seemed to recognize his family, but looked very pale and weak. The nurse put down the spoon she was using to feed her patient.

"Just ten minutes, everyone. That is all. He needs rest and quiet," she warned.

Margaret stepped to the back of the line hoping that against all odds, Russell might ask for her. She listened as everyone told Russell how glad they were that he had recovered. He never mentioned Margaret's name. So when her turn came, she smiled and did her best to act normal. Her stomach was churning.

"Russell, I'm glad you are awake," she said quietly. He offered her a sleepy smile in return.

The nurse came back with the doctor in tow. "Out, all you people. This is much too many," he barked. "Wait in the hall."

Before leaving, Margaret placed the sealed envelope on the table beside her husband's bed. He would see it later, and by then, she would be gone.

The family mingled happily in the hallway, assured of Russell's recovery. Margaret knew this might be her one chance to get away. Quickly, she thought up an excuse to leave. "I think I will go run a secret errand. I want to surprise Russell later today, now that he is well," she spoke in creative truths.

Joanna and Anna asked for details, but Margaret refused to offer anything. "Goodbye," she simply said, waving her hand as she walked down the hall.

Margaret paused around the corner to hold her throbbing head. Her emotions were running wild, and getting the best of her. She closed her eyes, trying not to cry. With slow but determined steps, she made her way down the stairs. In the foyer of the main lobby however, Margaret felt suddenly weak. It was difficult to breathe. The room began to spin too. Before she knew what was happening, Margaret collapsed onto the floor.

"Miss? Oh, miss?" a strange voice was calling from the fog in her head. Margaret let out a groan as her nose inhaled an awful stench.

"She's coming to, Doctor," the voice said.

Margaret's eyes fluttered open. A white-capped nurse was leaning over her holding a bottle of smelling salts. Margaret noticed she was lying on a bed in a small room. She must still be in the hospital.

"What happened?" she asked in a small voice.

"You fainted," the nurse answered.

"I did?" Margaret was horrified and embarrassed. She had never done that before.

The doctor leaned in closer. "Are your laces too tight, miss?" has asked quietly. "And do you faint often?"

"No. Never before," Margaret managed with a blush.

"Why do you think you fainted then?" he questioned.

Margaret thought about her crazy emotions this week. Actually, it was not surprising that she had fainted. She told a half-truth for an answer. "My husband is upstairs, Doctor. He was missing for a few days. I've been very upset..."

"What's your name, ma'am?"

"Missus Russell Chadwick."

"Missus Chadwick, could it be possible, that you are with child?" the doctor asked next.

His question hit Margaret like a runaway train. Surely not! She sat staring at him in stunned silence. Could it possibly be? No! "We've only been, uh, together, a few times, Doctor," she tried to explain.

"Madam, it only takes once," he replied without breaking a smile. "Better to know for sure."

An hour later, Margaret did not know whether to laugh or cry. She was indeed, carrying Russell's child. She was finally getting her wish to have a family, but oh, what terrible, terrible timing. Did this change things? Yes. But should she return to Russell? No. Every fiber in her being said no! But what could she do? She needed time, time to think about a new plan. Margaret's mind raced. She could go west, pretend to be a widow. Go back to the agency. Where could she go that was safe to think things over? Elsie's Boarding House.

With this one small piece to her plan, Margaret returned to the house to gather her things. Inside her bag was enough money for a month's rent at Elsie's. Yes. Elsie was a mother-figure. She would help Margaret figure out what to do. And in time, she and the baby would be just fine.

"Where is Margaret?" Russell asked from bed later that afternoon. He had so much to tell her. His parents had explained why he had been admitted to the hospital. Sadly, he could not remember it himself. He was so ashamed of his behavior. He owed Margaret an enormous apology. Apparently, news of Ethel's death had been too much for him to bear at the time, but now, somehow, through the shock of his own near death experience, he had come to terms with the past. Everything in his world took on a deeper meaning now.

Joanna hesitated to tell him, but he seemed so worried. "She's out right now son. I'm sure we will see her soon," she answered with a secretive twinkle in her eyes. Everyone grinned with the knowledge that she was out making special plans.

By nightfall however, no one was smiling. Henry and Anna had taken the boys home for the night, in hopes of finding Margaret there. But when they discovered that her trunk was missing, they immediately returned to the hospital.

"Where could she have gone?" Russell asked with sincere worry. He would go out and look for her himself, if he could. His body was not yet up to the task of walking, much less a full blown search party.

Not having any other ideas, Anna suggested, "Do you think she went back to Iowa?"

"That wouldn't make much sense, dear,. Her husband is here," Joanna concluded.

Russell looked away from his parents in shame as he absorbed his mother's remark. He knew what kind of a husband he had been. Not a very good one. His behavior had been reprehensible. May God, and Margaret, forgive him. "She didn't go home, Anna," Russell said slowly. "I'm sure she has left me. It's been a long time coming, and I deserve it."

There was a gasp in the room as everyone stared in shock. Only Henry seemed to understand. Russell felt an explanation was in order. "I was horrid to her. I've acted so terribly."

Joanna tried to soothe her son's obvious shame. "She did tell me about a few things, Russ honey. And you do have some apologizing to do, but really, it wasn't anything worth leaving you for."

Russell hung his head low. "Mother, I am sure you don't know half of it. She has every right to leave me. But if we can find her, I will beg her to take me back. She is so deserving."

Early the next morning, Russell found Margaret's letter. It had been hidden under his food tray the day before, and then was covered up with a newspaper for the rest of the day. When his family arrived, Russell shared all he knew. George launched a city-wide search, notifying the police and the newspapers. For two days, the family scouted the streets and train stations, the docks and the stagecoach offices. Joanna and Anna went by a dozen churches and notified friends of the family, just in case. Henry even inquired at other hospitals. But after two days, everyone grew discouraged. She had simply disappeared.

All the while, Russell remained in the hospital, helpless to offer assistance in the massive search for his wife. With his family away though, he had much time to think. He offered numerous prayers of apology, and asked God for Margaret's safe return. "I promise, things will be different," he whispered into the air.

Late on the second day, the family returned to the hospital. Each one gave an account, a report of the day's progress. After some thought, Russell announced, "She must still be in town then. You've all searched the depot and the stations and the docks. No one has seen her. So she is still here, hiding."

"I agree," Henry nodded.

"We should take out an ad in the paper and offer a reward, a good reward," Russell declared. "I'll pay fifty dollars for information."

And so it was agreed and arranged. George volunteered to stop by the newspaper office first thing in the morning. With luck, they could get the ad in tomorrow evening's paper.

"She just has to be found," Russell moaned from the bed. He loved her, he really did. If it was too late to tell her, what a fool he had been.

When the Chadwicks returned home from church Sunday morning, a telegram awaited them. Quickly, George opened the envelope and read the contents. "Johnny, run to the hospital and tell your brother that Margaret has been found!"

Russell was going to be released later in the afternoon. He would be able to go to her and plead for her return.

"Where is she?" Joanna asked impatiently.

"At a boarding house, Elsie's Boarding House, in Chicago," George answered. "Thank goodness!"

"Let's go get her!" Joanna stated with excitement.

George put his hand out. "Dear, that is Russell's job. This situation is between the two of them. He has to fix it. I'd like to give him the chance to make things right, without our interference. Besides, I have every faith that he will bring her back."

Johnny waited as his brother dressed. Speaking hastily with the nurse, he had insisted that he be released immediately. Russell signed the papers as fast as he could.

"Be sure to come see me in two days, Mister Chadwick," the doctor instructed. "And no strenuous activity. Rest and warmth."

"Yes sir." Russell answered. Once the doctor had left, the two brothers went quickly down the hall.

Russell hired a carriage to take them home. Russell knew he was not up to the long walk. He was weak even now, but determined to find his wife. He wanted to see her today.

When he reached home, he changed clothes, then left again right away. A carriage would take him to the station and a train would take him into the city. From there, he would hire a driver to reach the boarding house on Dearborn Street. With luck, he would be there within the hour.

Margaret heard footsteps coming up the stairs. She continued with her mending until someone knocked on the door.

"Come in," she called out, thinking it was her kind landlady. Margaret looked up with a smile, but lost it when Russell entered her safe little room. The breath left her body in shock. How did he find her?

"Margaret! I'm so glad I found you!" Russell said as he rushed into the room. He fell to his knees in front of his speechless wife. "I beg your forgiveness Margaret. I was wretched. Gastly! Please forgive me. Please? I'm so sorry for everything."

Margaret found her voice, although she was still visibly shaken by his presence. "Russell, how did you find me?"

"I was frantic with worry about you, the whole family was. We've been searching for days. My family went everywhere. We notified the police and put an ad in the paper. Someone recognized your description, and I'm so grateful. I have so much to tell you," he confessed.

Margaret waited. He had apologized before. He had lied before. "Go on then. Say what you have to say," she replied calmly.

Slowly, he began. "When I heard about Ethel, I went out of my mind. I was so upset. I blamed myself for letting her die because she was supposed to have been my wife. Even though she left me, I loved her to the depths of my soul. My heart and spirit broke when Daniel said what he did. My world, in my mind, crashed down around me and I was lost. That was why I left Iowa. I had to see her, or at least be near her once again. When I saw her grave and knew that she was truly gone, I sunk to my very lowest. I know this is no excuse for the way I treated you, but I can honestly tell you now that I am a changed man. Facing death, I realized how very precious life is. I was wasting away inside before all this happened. But now, my heart is free to love again. I've been released from a cage I had built around myself. God gave me a second chance, Margaret, and I need you. I love you. Please stay with me. Be my wife. We will be happy together. We have so much to live for."

Margaret thought about his words. He had said much, things she had longed to hear. And he seemed sincere, but, he had hurt her so many times before. Margaret was hesitant to blindly trust again. She dared not tell him about the baby, because then he would insist on her return. She wanted to have a choice, to decide for herself what to do. When she looked at him, she could see the hope in his eyes.

"Russell, I need some time. Let me think about it. I'll send word in a few days and give you an answer."

He frowned, but nodded. "I know I deserve this. You have every right to leave me." He took a deep breath as he stood to leave. "But know this Margaret, if you stay with me, you will be loved. I will never let you forget how much. I will love you always, even if you do leave me."

Margaret's eyes teared up at last, but she dared not speak.

"Please don't disappear again," Russell requested. "I will wait for your telegram. Let me know if you need anything." With these last words, he left her little rented room. His shoulders were slumped, his face forlorn. At least she had not laughed in his face, or kicked him out of the room.

As Russell waited on the sidewalk for a carriage, he knew he might never see his wife again. It broke his heart. She could disappear forever and it would be his fault entirely.

The following evening, Russell paced the floor of his parent's home. He was so anxious to hear from Margaret, the wait was tearing him up inside. It was exhausting, and gave him an awful headache. He was weak, both emotionally and physically.

"Russ, you look pale," Joanna observed from her chair in the parlor. He had told her everything. Together, they and the rest of the family were praying for a good outcome, a good answer from Margaret. "You should sit."

"Pacing won't help, Son, trust me," George said from his sofa. Curls of smoke drifted toward the ceiling from his pipe. A newspaper hid his face.

Russell wondered how his father always seemed to remain so calm in any crisis. It was amazing. He did take a seat, only to have his fretting mother walk over and place the back of her hand on his forehead. Honestly, she was babying him like a mother hen. He was a grown man for crying out loud.

"I'm fine, Mother!" he spoke rudely. "Just worried about Margaret."

"You're not fine. Your fever is back," she stated. "George, take this boy back to the hospital immediately."

Not finding the strength to fight his mother's command, Russell allowed his father to drive him back to the doctors. George explained the situation and two men helped Russell into a bed. George signed paperwork while the physician examined the patient.

"You say you were released yesterday?" the mustached man asked.

Russell nodded.

"Have you been resting today?" was the next question.

Russell looked toward his father. The doctor knew by the lack of response that the answer was 'no.' "Young man, you are ill again because you are not staying in bed. You need rest, and lots of it.

You must eat and sleep only for another week. Nothing else, understand?"

Russell nodded again.

The doctor sent the nurse out for some medicine to reduce the fever. He then took the papers from George. "It says here your name is Russell Chadwick," the doctor stated.

"Yes sir," he answered.

"Well, congratulations to you! I had the privilege of meeting your wife several days ago. Quite a pretty lady she is too. Seems to me you would want to stay home and let her tend to you. Just see that she doesn't do too much work in the condition she's in."

Russell frowned. "What condition?"

"Your wife? Didn't she tell you?"

"Tell me what?" Russell demanded. If Margaret was sick, he needed to know. He sat up in the bed, awake and alert.

"Oh dear... I've done it again!" the doctor huffed. "My apologies sir, for spoiling the surprise."

Russell was growing impatient. "Doctor, please!" he nearly shouted. "What is wrong with my wife?"

The doctor laughed a short chuckle. "Nothing is wrong with her, sir. She is with child, that's all," he said finally.

Russell's eyes opened wide. "What?" he asked rhetorically. "A baby? Are you sure?"

"Quite sure. She's due late summer."

Russell could hardly believe it. Yes it was possible, but certainly not probable. "Um, you sure you have the right woman? Red hair, pretty skin, curvy..."

The doctor nodded. "That's the one."

Russell stared at the doctor, then at his father. "A baby?" Then a slow smile spread on his face. And he smiled so much he nearly laughed. "A baby!"

"Oh but your mother is going to be thrilled," George declared to his son.

"We have to go to her, Father, right now," Russell told him. His father nodded in agreement.

"Take this first, sir," the nurse requested. She had just arrived with his medications.

"And remember to rest!" the doctor ordered again.

Knowing that the train between Wheaton and Chicago would not run again until morning, George steered the carriage east. It was only ten miles to the city limits. Setting the horses at a quick trot, they would be there in no time.

"I can't believe she didn't tell me about the baby, Pa," Russell whispered while they were on their way.

"Can't you?" George spoke frankly. "She doesn't trust you, Son. Can't say I don't blame her."

Russell stared at his shoes. His father was right. Margaret didn't trust him, she had no reason to. He had deceived her far too many times. What a mess he had made of things. If only she would give him another chance. He would make things right. He simply had to, for the child's sake.

The courthouse clock struck nine as George led the team through town. It was bitter cold outside, but at least the stars were out. There would be no snow tonight. With Russell's directions, George found the boarding house without any trouble along the gas lit streets.

They both walked up the steps, but Russell knocked on the door. It took a few moments, but a man finally answered. "All the rooms are taken tonight," he announced to his visitors.

"We're not here for a room," Russell stated. "I need to see my wife, Margaret, if you please. Missus Russell Chadwick."

The man stepped back and allowed the men to enter. George took a soft seat in the parlor and warmed himself near the fire. "I'll just wait here," he told his son. Russell and Margaret had to work this out privately. And in the meantime, he thought about how to tell his wife that she was going to be a grandmother. How grand! Just the thought of her surprise made him smile.

Russell climbed the steps to Margaret's room and tapped softly on the door. "Margaret, it's me," he spoke gently. "Russell. I need to talk with you, please."

For a moment, there was only silence, but then he heard shuffling feet. Margaret opened the door wearing only a nightgown. Her room inside was toasty warm. From the look in her eyes, it was obvious that she had been sleeping. Her long red hair was disheveled down her back.

"What are you doing here?" she asked with irritation. "I told you I would send you my answer."

"May I come in?" he asked.

She glared angrily for several seconds, but then opened the door. "Be quick Russell, I'm very tired."

Russell took a deep breath. He had to do this right. He couldn't blow it. He moved slowly and reached for her hand. The room was lit only by the orange flames in the fireplace, but he could see so many emotions on her face. "Margaret, darling, is there anything that you want to tell me?"

Margaret frowned. She had spent the entire day trying to decide on her answer. Even still, she had none to give. She shook her head.

Russell looked into her eyes. "Margaret, I know about the baby. I wish you would have told me," he said calmly.

Margaret's heart sank into her feet. How did he find out? How? He wasn't supposed to know. That would ruin everything!

"Why wouldn't you tell me?" he asked. "I'm so excited. I'm ecstatic!"

A small sob escaped Margaret's throat. All of her fears and fretting and planning over her future seemed to be crumbling. This wasn't part of the plan. Why was Russell being so kind, so nice? So... loving?

In a blink, Russell's arms were wrapped around her upper body. "Baby, I love you! I love you, Margaret Chadwick," he said, emphasizing her name. "My ghosts are all gone, I swear. You are the woman God had planned for me all along, I was just too blind and stupid to see it. But my eyes are open now. I see what a wonderful woman you are. I see the mother of my child, my children. Please baby, stay with me." He gave her body a gentle squeeze. "And please, please forgive me for all the awful things I said and did. I know I caused you pain and misery. It won't happen again, I swear."

Margaret simply stood as tears slid from her eyes.

At last, Russell pulled away and held both her shoulders gently. "I want you, Margaret. I want this baby, our baby. I want you to come home with me. But, if you just can't live with me, then my parents want you to live with them. You will always be a part of this family, and you will always have a home with us. Don't leave. Please, don't leave." He had to close his eyes at his last request. The thought of her disappearing with his child was just too much.

Margaret was so full of emotions, she felt almost nauseated. Part of her wanted so badly to believe him, to give in. But… she just didn't know.

He begged again. "Just try it. Stay with me for one week. If you're miserable, I'll bring you to my parent's house."

Margaret wiped her eyes and found her voice. "All I ever wanted from you Russell, was your love," she whispered.

"I know. And you have it. Until the day I die," he replied sincerely.

Margaret's hand fell down to her abdomen. She thought about the child. The tiny life inside her body deserved a father. As a deep calming breath of warm air filled her lungs, she finally nodded. "I will try," she conceded. "You have one month to convince me."

Russell smiled and sighed with relief. Then he hugged her gratefully. "You will never doubt it again, my darling. I love you, I love you, I love you!"

Epilogue

"It's a girl!" Susan shouted from the top of the stairs.

Russell nearly jumped out of his skin with excitement. "Can I see her?" he asked impatiently.

Susan grinned. "Come on up!"

Russell took the stairs two at a time.

"Hair just like her mother's" Susan boasted proudly.

Russell anxiously stepped into the bedroom at the top of the landing. The last ten hours downstairs had been pure torture for him. He had been praying fervently for Margaret's life and the baby's life too. Knowing Ethel had died trying to bring life into the world made this day all the more worrisome. But God had answered his prayers, and spared his wife and child. For that, Russell was eternally grateful. Margaret and this baby girl meant the world to him. They were his life, his very purpose for being.

"A girl, Margaret. With red hair too. How wonderful. I'm so proud of you," he spoke with a grateful heart. He looked first at his wife and then at the tiny bundle. The little girls' eyes were blue, and seemed so knowing and wise as she stared at him. Russell was overcome with emotions, his eyes watered. She was beautiful, amazing and wonderful all in one.

Margaret looked tired and weak. But she was more beautiful than ever. "You're a momma now," he smiled proudly. She smiled weakly, absolutely drained from the delivery.

But Margaret was happy. She was glad to give Russell a daughter. He had been true to his word of last December, and had loved her every moment of every day since. The months leading up to this long August day had been the best of her life so far. Russell had insisted on pampering her during the entire pregnancy. He had helped prepare meals, made beds, washed linens, swept floors and even served her breakfast in bed on occasion. Then during the gentle summer evenings, they had sat on the front porch and held hands. It was a special time for them both, watching the corn sway on the wind in every field and watching ripples on the river.

At church socials, Russell had danced with her and presented her proudly at every event. When her stomach grew large, he made sure she had clothes that fit, and helped her get in and out of chairs. He had even, on occasion, held her stomach and sung to the child inside. But best of all, every night when they went to bed, Russell told Margaret, "I love you." It made her heart melt, because this time, he meant it.

Their love was growing stronger by the day, but today, it seemed, was the height of love. They had a child now, a sweet daughter to share. Margaret watched Russell's face as he cradled their baby. Rebecca Joy Chadwick was her name; they had agreed on that months ago.

"I love you, Rebecca," Russell whispered before he placed a kiss on the newborn's forehead. "And I love your momma too." He smiled and glanced down at Margaret. "And in time, we will give you brothers and sisters to play with, and you'll grow up happy and strong."

Margaret grinned. Yes, she had made the right decision. She was loved. Russell was everything she had ever hoped for. She would stay with him forever. And one day, years from now, out in that little graveyard behind the house, they would lie side by side. No one would know what odds they had overcome, but their love would endure for all eternity.

*What's in
YOUR
purse?*

*Iris, David,
Hattie, Barney
& more: a story
of God's love.*

MORE FROM ENERGION PUBLICATIONS

Fiction

Covenant	Daniel Martin	$17.99
Megabelt	Nick May	$12.99
Prayer Trilogy	Kimberly Gordon	$9.99
Stories of the Way	Henry Neufeld	$9.99
The Traveler's Advance	Heath Taws	$14.99
Allegheny Hideaway	Kimberly Gordon	$16.99

Personal Study

Holy Smoke! Unholy Fire	Bob McKibben	$14.99
The Jesus Paradigm	David Alan Black	$17.99
The Sacred Journey	Chris Surber	$12.99
When People Speak for God	Henry Neufeld	$17.99

Christian Living

Grief: Finding the Candle of Light	Jody Neufeld	$8.99
I Want to Pray	Perry M. Dalton	$7.99
It's in the Bag	Kimberly Gordon	$5.99
Soup Kitchen for the Soul	Renee Crosby	$12.99
Crossing the Street	Robert LaRochelle	$16.99

Bible Study

Learning and Living Scripture	Lentz/Neufeld	$12.99
Luke: A Participatory Study Guide	Geoffrey Lentz	$8.99
Philippians: A Participatory Study Guide	Bruce Epperly	$9.99
Ephesians: A Participatory Study Guide	Robert D. Cornwall	$9.99

Theology

The Politics of Witness	Allan R. Bevere	$9.99
Ultimate Allegiance	Robert D. Cornwall	$9.99
Gomorrah Was Religious Too	Chris Surber	$9.99
The Church Under the Cross	William Powell Tuck	$11.99
Journey to the Undiscovered Country	William Powell tuck	$9.99

Generous Quantity Discounts Available

Dealer Inquiries Welcome

Energion Publications — P.O. Box 841

Gonzalez, FL_ 32560

Website: http://energionpubs.com

Phone: (850) 525-3916